Georgia Griebel Gates

Bistro Hunting Mystery

A Baker Street Bistro Mystery

Bistro Hunting Mystery

Cover design by Pat Bodkin
Edited by Dianne Poston Owens

This book is a work of fiction. Any resemblance to actual persons or events is purely coincidental.

Other books by Georgia Griebel Gates

Baker Street Bistro Mysteries:
Baker Street Bistro
Bistro Swamp Mystery
Bistro Bourbon Mystery
Bistro Guild Mystery
Bistro Christmas Mystery

Visit us on Facebook: Baker Street Bistro Mysteries
Visit our website: bakerstreetbistromysteries.com

Sign Up for the Baker Street Bistro Mysteries Monthly Newsletter on either our website or Facebook page to get book updates, recipes, and more!

Chapter One

Fall and cooler weather had arrived. Let me rephrase that. The month of September had arrived, and since I live in South Carolina somewhat cooler weather had arrived with it. The change in temperature made me want to go outside and plant fall flowers, maybe take a walk along the boardwalk, or explore the park. Instead, I was stuck in my tiny office at our family business, the Baker Street Bistro, processing payroll and paying invoices. It didn't look like I would be taking walks in the park any time soon because when I was done, I had to do network operating system updates. Somehow my life had become much busier since I retired. My part time jobs had morphed into a full time job. Besides being bookkeeper and IT person for our two restaurants and our coffee shop and bakery, I work as an IT consultant for the Blue River Police Department, the Sheriff's Department, the Blue River Art Guild, and the Irons' Estate.

I was debating taking a coffee break when I got a text message from my sister-in-law, Ellie. Her text said, "Mavis and Mo are here. They asked about you."

That was the only excuse I needed to head next door to the coffee shop. I crossed the foyer separating the two businesses and went directly to the espresso machine to fix myself a latte. Ellie was working the machine.

"Gracie, glad you could come over. I'll fix your latte if you deliver these drinks. I've got them labeled, and yes, your father-in-law is actually drinking a mocha."

I picked up the drink tray and headed to the group lounging in the seating area by the front windows. What a group it was! Mavis and Mo Baxter, owners of a coffee roasting business in nearby Beaufort, were laughing and talking to Gator Joe Johnson, a former moonshiner turned legitimate distillery owner, and my father-in-law, Big Frank Alderman, retired farmer and current city council chairman. The fact that my father-in-law and Gator Joe were drinking mochas in a coffee shop would never cease to amaze me.

Mavis Baxter jumped up to help me pass out the drinks. "Miss Gracie, glad you're here. I was afraid you'd be too busy to visit."

"I can always spare a little time to visit with you. How are you doing? You look great!"

"Oh, Girl, thanks, though I'm not quite a hundred percent. My hair has grown back some and I'm even gettin' used to this stupid ostomy bag, but I still get worn out after a day at the shop."

"It hasn't been a year yet. Didn't the doctor say it would take at least a year to recover, even without the chemo? And look at you! You're able to go to the shop. That's great!"

We sat down with the gentlemen and joined in a lively conversation about local politics, which changed to national issues, and digressed into a debate over the last Darlington race and NASCAR standings. In self-defense, Mavis and I began our own side conversation about our children.

Mavis and I had just about finished updates on all our kids when my phone rang.

The caller ID showed it was my brother-in-law, known to the family as Little Frank. Since he is also the Sheriff, I decided I'd better take the call and excused myself. Unfortunately the connection was poor. His voice faded in and out. He must have been experiencing the same problem on his end, because the few words that were loud and clear were expletives. The call ended.

I went into the foyer so the coffee shop noise wouldn't be an issue and started to call Frank back when I got a call with the Sheriff's Department ID.

Answering it, I expected to hear my brother-in-law; instead I heard my daughter, Lucy. "Hey, Mom, Uncle Frank wants you to tell someone from South Carolina Law Enforcement Division how to get to Mill Pond Road. I think he said it was Lieutenant Richardson. He said the SLED guy would stop at the Bistro in a few minutes."

"Okay. What's going on at Mill Pond Road?"

"I think it's a hunting accident. It was hard to understand everything even over the police radio. You know how flaky the reception is in that area. I guess there was no cell reception at all."

I bid good-bye to my coffee shop pals and headed back to my office. I had no more than sat down at my desk when the SLED Lieutenant entered.

Without preamble Richardson said, "Can you tell me why so many places around here can't be found using GPS? Where in the heck is Mill Pond Road? I don't even see it on a local map."

"In this particular case the real name of the road is Miller's Pond Road, but the first road sign was misspelled. It's been misspelled on all the subsequent signs. For some reason the signs are stolen regularly too, which doesn't help. The locals just started calling it Mill Pond Road rather than fighting the issue. As far as the problem with GPS, the cell tower closest to that area has been hit by lightning one time too many. Reception has been flaky there for years."

Lieutenant Richardson had such a scowl on his face, I had to add, "Elmer Grub has his own theory about the bad reception. He thinks an alien space craft is buried in the hill behind the pond."

"Of course it is! So how do I get to this Mill Pond Road or Miller's Pond Road, whatever it's called?"

"You know where Carter's Corner Store is?"

"Please don't tell me I have to go over Grub's Bridge Road to get there."

"No, no! You will have to drive past that road though. When you get to the store, set your trip meter to 12.5 miles and head northeast."

I took out a piece of printer paper and drew a tiny store in one corner and sketched in landmarks as I talked. "At 12.5 miles you'll see a road, Grumpy's Shortcut. That sign has been stolen so many times I doubt they even try to replace it anymore. In any case, you'll recognize that intersection because there's a red brick house on the corner. It has white trim, a black roof, a chain link fence, and there's usually a couple of semis in the yard. If the semis aren't there, they'll have a couple of trailers parked in the yard for sure. Turn right on Grumpy's Shortcut. For goodness sake, don't go left."

Richardson just shook his head.

"Grumpy's Shortcut meanders around a bit. You'll come across two forks in the road. At the first one, you take the left fork. At the second one, take the right fork, but slow down. I mean go very slow! The folks who live in the white house have free range animals. They have three or four dachshunds, chickens, ducks, and a couple of goats. I've even seen a pig running loose, although, come to think of it, that might have been a wild hog. It's a real zoo."

"Kind of like your backyard then?" said Richardson.

"The animals in my backyard belong to our neighbor and Debbie keeps all her animals contained behind a tall fence. Part of it is our fence, but the animals are contained at all times."

"Right! So where do I go after I get past the zoo?"

"When you pass the house, set your trip meter to 9.7 miles. As you get closer to Mill Pond Road, you'll see tall stands of long leaf pine on both sides of the road and cattails in the drainage ditches. At 9.7 miles the trees on the left end abruptly. Mill Pond Road is on the left. Since it's a dirt road, it's easy to miss. They don't always keep it scraped off. The last time I drove out that way, there was a field of cotton on the right side of Mill Pond Road, but that was last year's cotton, so they may have harvested it or plowed it under by now. You aren't driving one of those little white sedans are you, Lieutenant?"

"No, I've got a Jeep like Frank has. Why?"

"It's been raining. Mill Pond Road is dirt with some dips and holes here and there. You might have to drive in the field or hug the tree line to get around them. You should be okay with a Jeep."

"Terrific!"

"One more thing, when you get to the actual pond, the road branches. If you go left, it will take you to a parking area. It's down wind normally, so hunters like to park there. If you go right, the road goes up hill toward the tree line and kind of peters out."

As I finished my little discourse, I handed the lieutenant the map I'd drawn and added, "It's not to scale, but I've drawn in all the landmarks."

Richardson studied the map, shook his head, and said, "Thanks for the directions."

"Would you like bottled water to take with you? It's supposed to get warm this afternoon."

"No, thanks. I've got a couple of bottles in the Jeep."

After the Lieutenant left, I went back to the coffee shop, made myself a second latte, and rejoined Mavis. The men had switched topics to football, so we continued our own discussion.

"So Max and Bud are at paramedic training for the week?" Mavis asked.

"Yes, they both want to keep up their certification. They don't do a regular rotation anymore. They just help out when there's an emergency or when the fire department is short handed."

"I don't know how y'all do it. Workin' two or three jobs like that," Mavis said.

"Max and Bud decided to retire from their paramedic jobs when the business expanded. Max has had to cut back on his chef duties too, since he took over the administration of his mother's trust. And that's a shame too. He loves cooking and too often the charitable trust creates a paperwork nightmare."

"What about you? How many jobs are you workin'?" Mavis asked.

"Since Lucy has been working in the Sheriff's department IT division, I haven't had to do quite as much there. She even helps me at the Blue River Police Department sometimes."

We continued our visit until Mo looked at his watch and announced that they'd better head back to Beaufort. They had about a half hour drive and he wanted to get back to their shop by lunch time.

Once again in my office, I finished payroll. Just as the last of the database information was transmitted and requisite funds moved over, another phone call came from the sheriff's department.

"Sorry to bother you again, Mom, but Uncle Frank called again. He would like you to pick up the Hardy boys and deliver them to Miller's Pond. Who are the Hardy boys? Are they locals?"

"Oh, he's talking about the two SLED officers, Glenbrook and Samuelson. For some reason, they remind him of the Hardy boys, you know, from the mystery stories."

Lucy was silent for a minute, then she said, "I guess if you ignore the fact that Officer Glenbrook is black, they are kind of like the Hardy boys, aren't they?"

"Your dad said the very same thing! But the Lieutenant is definitely not like Fenton Hardy."

"No, he sure isn't!"

As soon as I disconnected, I tossed my gear into my tote, locked the office, grabbed a twelve pack of bottled water, and headed out to my Suburban. I didn't want to keep the Hardy boys waiting.

Officers Glenbrook and Samuelson didn't look thrilled when I pulled up in front of Carter's Corner Store about a half hour later. I got out and opened the rear doors of my Suburban.

"You may have to put some of your gear in the second seat. My husband took out the third seat and had this gun safe bolted to the frame. Max wanted me to have a secure place for our rifles and my police gear. We also carry a change of clothes, waders, boots, blankets, and a cooler. Oh, and one of my husband's paramedic kits."

"And a couple bags of cat litter," Samuelson said.

"All you need is some food and you'd be good to go anywhere," Glenbrook said.

"From past experience, I can understand why you carry waders and a change of clothes," Samuelson added.

While the SLED officers loaded their gear in the back of my Suburban, I went inside the store and purchased a couple bags of ice for my cooler and more water, just to be safe.

Once we were on the road, Glenbrook asked, "Are we going across Grub's Bridge by chance?"

"No, we'll go past that road, but we won't be crossing that bridge."

"That's a relief!"

His relief was short lived. Once we pulled off the highway onto Mill Pond Road, things got tricky. As predicted, the road had several dips and holes filled with water. I had to drive off road, either edging the field on the right or hugging the tree line on the left in order to get past.

"Mrs. Alderman, please tell me why we always run into water when we ride with you?"

"I believe you get stuck riding with me because there's water involved."

Both men were gritting their teeth as we made our way along the road to the pond. When we reached the spot where the road branched, I went left. As we rounded the pond, the pine trees gave way to a clearing and we could see a myriad of law enforcement vehicles filling the crude parking area. Finding a place to park was difficult, but I managed to squeeze my Suburban between the sheriff's department forensic van and my brother-in-law's big Jeep.

When we climbed out of my vehicle, Frank greeted us. "I see you arrived safe and sound."

"At least we didn't have to swim," Glenbrook said.

"Your lieutenant said to put your gear by his Jeep. It's parked on the other side of the van. Richardson is over by the spot where our victim fell," Frank said.

While we watched the officers unload their gear from my Suburban, I said, "I have bottled water in the cooler if anyone needs it."

"I could use some right now. I'll spread the word."

After Frank got his water, I asked, "So what happened here, Frank?"

"The two hunters who found the body thought the guy was shot in a hunting accident. We're pretty sure it wasn't an accident."

"How is that? Isn't this deer season? Or is it archery only at this point."

"This is private land, so it doesn't matter. The fact that our victim was shot twice, one of those shots being at close range, makes me think he was killed on purpose. I'm also suspicious because the victim was supposed to meet with Lieutenant Richardson tomorrow afternoon."

"That does put a different spin on things, doesn't it. Who's the victim?"

"Vance Treblek."

"Is he the father of the young woman who disappeared a couple years ago?

"One and the same. He phoned Richardson a couple days ago to say he had some new information that might lead to his daughter's killer."

"Then he was sure his daughter is dead?"

"Yep! Of course we still haven't found a body. If you remember, searchers thought they found something shortly after she disappeared. A cadaver dog kept signaling a find in the water at Swamp Lake. Unfortunately the bottom was too muddy and divers couldn't find anything. Treblek wanted them to drain the swamp. Made a big stink about it, but Swamp Lake is way too big to drain."

"I can understand why he was so adamant about that and persistent in his efforts to find justice. It's hard when you don't know what's happened to a loved one. There's no closure."

"Detective Andrews went over to Treblek's house and searched the place. Carlton also talked to the ex-wife. She said Vance was at the Blue River Tavern last night for dinner. While he was sitting at the bar, Treblek announced that he planned to go hunting early this morning.

"Say, Gracie, if you have the time and since you've been so helpful before, could you help us out here? We're short handed, since we have the Fall Festival to cover. We didn't find any brass near the body. We're searching for the spot where the killer fired his first shot."

Given the choice between processing mounds of paperwork in my office or tromping around Miller's Pond searching for shell casings, I opted for the sunshine and fresh air.

"Okay, Frank. I'll stay and help. Where do you want me to start?"

"We've got teams on the left side of the pond working the tree line. Why don't you head around to the right. Junior's over that way."

I met up with my nephew as he was searching along the road, just inside the tree line. Junior had been a member of the Blue River Police Department since he graduated college. He had also recently applied to the FBI. We were all anxious to hear if he'd been accepted.

"Hey, Aunt Gracie. They drag you here to help?"

"I drove Glenbrook and Samuelson here," I said. "Found anything yet?"

"Nope. I don't think this would be a good

spot for a shot. The bank around the pond is too high. You'd be lucky to see the target's head from this location."

I turned around to look in the direction of the parking lot where the body was found. We could see the tops of vehicles, but not the spot where the body had lain. It had been marked with short flags, but those weren't visible at all.

"The other side of the pond would be better," I said. "It would be a straighter shot. On the other hand, it looks like the shooter might be visible to their target unless it was very dark. There's not much undergrowth to hide a person in that stretch, even if he was wearing camo gear. Around the pond on the hill end might be even better. There's more undergrowth there. A shooter would be looking down on the target. Of course that would be a long shot for sure."

"You could make a shot like that, couldn't you? Especially if you used that nice Viper scope Uncle Max bought for you," he asked.

"I might have been able to make a three hundred yard shot when I was younger. My eyes aren't what they used to be, and Max and I haven't had time to go to the range." After I thought about the shot for a minute, I said, "Actually, if I was making the shot at dawn, I'd use Max's scope. It's a Bushnell and it's supposed to be better in low light."

We continued to search along the tree line, going further and further up the hill, until we were directly opposite the location of the body on the other side of the pond. When I turned around to look toward the parking lot, I could see the flags marking the spot clearly.

"Aunt Gracie, take a look at this."

I joined Junior beside a fallen tree a few feet into the woods.

"What do you have there?"

"I think someone smokes an awful lot. Look at that pile of cigarette butts."

"Someone was sitting here a long time, that's for sure. Whoever it was didn't field-strip their butts, did they? Looks like they ate something too," I said. "There's a plastic sandwich bag in the dirt."

"If this is the shooter's trash and he stayed here long enough to smoke all those cigarettes and eat, I wonder if he had to do something else."

While Junior waited for the sheriff's forensic team, I searched the area for another fallen log, perhaps a little further into the woods. By the time the forensic folks arrived, I had found another log and it had another pile of possible evidence. Junior came up beside me.

"Do you think that's human?" he asked.

"Either that or a large animal, but I don't think it's from a black bear. Their scat usually has bits of what they've been eating in it. It definitely doesn't look like any wild hog scat that I've seen. Doesn't seem likely it was a large dog. Could be a coyote, I suppose, but there's no fur in it."

I pulled out my cell phone and took a couple photos of the scat as well as the surrounding area and sent the photos to one of the medical examiners.

"Dr. Sykes is an expert on fecal material. He can tell us if it's animal droppings and what type of animal it was, but he likes to examine the scat in situ, as it were. He likes to do a chemical analysis of the feces, too. I hope my photos give him enough clues."

"Maybe I'd better get those forensic guys over here to collect the sample. I'll call Uncle Frank."

Chapter Two

The forensic team was not thrilled about the prospect of scooping scat. They had collected much worse over the years, so I didn't feel too sorry for them. While they worked on collecting evidence, Lieutenant Richardson and my brother-in-law discussed the situation.

"Frank, I know we haven't found anything anywhere else, but this seems like an awful long shot, in more ways than one. It would take a very good marksman to make a three hundred plus yard shot," Richardson said.

"Maybe that's why the killer had to take a second shot," Frank said. "And I've got two people standing right here who could make that long shot."

"You do?"

"Both Junior and Gracie can do it. Gracie, you got your rifles with you?" Frank asked.

My instinct was to deny it, but Junior knew I had the rifles and he deserved a chance to make that shot, so he could prove Frank's point. Whether I could make it was another matter.

"Junior, go with Gracie and see if you can set up some kind of target in the area where the body was found. I'll have the area cleared while you're doing that," Frank said.

Frank got busy on his police radio.

"I'm not sure what I can use for a target," Junior said as we tromped down the hill.

"I've got a bag of cat litter and a change of clothes. Maybe we could prop the bag up with sticks and put a t-shirt over it."

That's what we did. It looked funny, but it was probably about the same size as a human torso.

I grabbed my rifle, a box of ammo, and two binoculars. When we arrived back on top of the hill, I tried to calm myself down a little. It had been awhile since I'd done any shooting with a rifle. I was used to my Glock, since I went to the range with Lucy frequently, but shooting the rifle was different.

I handed Frank the binoculars. He handed one set to the Lieutenant. Frank used his police radio to tell everyone in the area to stay clear, then he said, "Whenever you're ready, guys."

I opted to go first. Even with my old eyes I could see the target through my scope just fine. There was no wind, so I didn't have to compensate for that. There would be a drop in trajectory, but I had enough target that I should be all right. I slowed my breathing, aimed, and on the exhale fired.

"I'd say she hit the target, wouldn't you?" Frank said.

I handed my rifle to Junior. He chambered a new round and took aim. When he fired, we could see another puff of dust and another hole opened up in the bag of litter.

"Looks like two for two, wouldn't you say?" Frank said.

Richardson scowled, handed Frank the binoculars, and said, "Mind if I try a shot?"

Junior handed him the rifle. After a minute, Richardson fired.

"Three for three! I think we can safely say that a shot from here is possible."

"If the shooter was waiting here for

Treblek, would he have hidden his car near the road?"

"The road that branches around the right side of the pond runs into the trees just over yonder. Maybe we should take a look. A person could hide their vehicle in the underbrush," Frank said.

Frank and the Lieutenant took off toward the spot where the road ended in the woods. Junior and I stayed behind and watched the forensic folks comb the area. The setting sun created shadows which made it hard to see. One of them shouted, "Bingo! Found a shell casing."

Junior and I walked to where Frank and Richardson were standing in time to hear Frank say, "It's going to be dark before we can get a good look around this section. I'll station some deputies here to keep people from entering the area and we can resume our search tomorrow."

"You're right. I do think this looks like a good spot to hide a vehicle. Those broken branches and the mashed down underbrush sure look like someone drove through here. With all the vehicles that have been in the area of the car park, we aren't going to find anything useful there."

While the Sheriff and Lieutenant Richardson talked about their strategy for the following day, I decided it was time to head back to Blue River. It was late and I was worn out from all the fresh air and exercise. I told Junior I was heading home and started down the overgrown remnants of the road. About half way to the parking area by the pond, I heard someone running downhill behind me. I turned to see Junior coming toward me.

"Hey, Aunt Gracie! Detective Andrews just called. He had to take the Chief to the hospital. Her water broke. I guess the baby is coming."

"Sunny did say she was ready to have the baby. Oh my gosh! Coach is in Charleston. I hope he can get back in time for the birth."

"Detective Andrews said he would stay with the Chief until her husband arrived. That should mean Coach is on the way to Beaufort Memorial."

"Maybe I'd better head over there. Sunny is probably stressed about this shooting. Someone from her town being shot is something she would take personally," I said. "Sunny's mom could calm her down, but I'm sure her mom is watching little Tiffany."

"You've got the Chief pegged. I'm supposed to head back to the station and manage things until Detective Andrews gets back. Hate to say it, but that's going to make us even more short-handed than we've been. They have most of the off duty officers scheduled to help at the Fall Festival. Frank's got deputies there already."

Instead of heading home, I headed to Beaufort Memorial Hospital. I changed my wet shoes to dry ones. I would have preferred to change my slacks, too. They were wet around the cuffs, but there was no convenient place to do that.

When I arrived at the hospital's labor and delivery unit, I found Detective Carlton Andrews standing in the hallway.

"How are things going?"

"The doctor is examining Sunny," Carlton

said. "Her contractions were five minutes apart during our trip here, and Sunny's stressed because she thinks we should be investigating that murder. You know she was going to drive herself to the hospital. How would she manage that?"

"Max and Bud had to take her to the hospital in their ambulance when she had her little girl. That was a couple years ago when we had that flooding. They said Sunny fussed at them the whole way. She thought they should be taking care of flood victims. Didn't do any good to argue that she was a flood victim too."

When the doctor and nurse came out of the room, Carlton and I went inside in time to see Sunny having a big contraction.

After the pain subsided some, Sunny said, "Oh, Miss Gracie, I'm glad to see you. Doesn't this beat all? My babies seem to have the worst timing."

"Can't be helped, Sunny. Babies come when they come. You know that. Besides there are plenty of folks to work on the investigation if that's what's worrying you," I said.

"Maybe you could stay and hold my hand until Coach gets here? That way Carlton can go talk to Treblek's buddies."

Both Sunny and Carlton looked relieved when I agreed to stay.

After Carlton left, Sunny said, "It's not just that I want him to go back to work. I don't think he was very comfortable with this whole labor business. Every time I had a contraction I thought he was going to have one, either that or a heart attack. I told him I could take myself to the hospital."

Sunny started to pant and I realized she was having another contraction. Breathlessly she said, "It doesn't help that my water pours out with each contraction. I hate to see what the passenger seat on my Jeep looks like."

After the contraction passed, Sunny said, "Max told me you drove yourself to the hospital once. Was that with John?"

"It was. My water broke too, but I wasn't having strong contractions. What I was feeling was more like false labor. I may have had a backache. It's been awhile. My memory has faded some. Anyway, I wouldn't have tried it if I was having contractions like you're having. I didn't have my first big one until I was in Beaufort. Had to pull my truck over until it passed. After my water broke, I had time to call my neighbor Debbie to come over to watch the kids, call the doctor, and call the fire department dispatcher. Debbie came right over. The doctor's office told me to head to the hospital, and the dispatcher told me Max and Bud were delivering a baby, so they wouldn't be available for awhile. That was in the dark ages before everyone had cell phones, so I just told the dispatcher I'd call back later."

"You didn't mind being here at the hospital by yourself?"

"No, John was baby number five. I'd been through it all before and knew my way around labor and delivery. Max showed up in time for John's arrival though. That was nice."

"I hope Coach gets here safe and sound. He kind of panicked when I called him. He was worried the baby was coming late and would be too big for me to deliver naturally. I told him it was only two weeks. A couple weeks either way is pretty normal, right?"

"It is."

Before I could say anything more, Sunny started having another contraction. "Talk to me. That helps. Tell me about Miller's Pond."

"Well, Treblek's body was found a few yards away from his truck. He must have been heading to the pond to check it out. Funniest thing though, they didn't find a rifle or shotgun with him. He had a new Wicked Ridge crossbow in his truck, but it was still in the box.

"Treblek had been shot twice. One of the shots was at close range. The forensic folks didn't find any shell casings by the body, so Frank had his team search along the tree line on the left side of the pond. That's left if you're standing in the car park looking at the pond. Junior and I searched the right side where the road goes up hill. If you remember that area, it's lower than the bank of the pond, so Junior figured it wasn't a likely spot for the shooter.

"Junior and I moved further up hill until we were directly across the pond from the spot where the body was found. It's got to be more than three hundred yards, but Junior found some possible evidence. It was cigarette butts. Lots of them. We also found a plastic sandwich bag. The forensic guys think it held a peanut butter and jelly sandwich. While the forensic team gathered that evidence, I looked around and found some scat. I photographed the pile and sent the pictures to Dr. Sykes. The forensic guys collected that too. It might be animal scat, but it was close to the cigarette butts."

Sunny's contraction subsided, but she was

still a little breathless when she spoke. "Treblek's ex said he planned to get to the pond by dawn. Whoever shot him had to get to Miller's Pond some time during the night if they wanted to beat Treblek there. You said there was a pile of cigarette butts? If they're any indication, that person must have been on site for several hours, maybe all night."

"All night would make sense," I said. "Finding a good spot for an ambush would best be done in daylight unless the person was very familiar with the area. Come to think of it, whoever shot Treblek had to know the area well enough to find Miller's Pond. That's private property and Old Miller doesn't let just anyone hunt on his land."

"You're right. It's not on any maps."

"And Richardson couldn't find it using GPS," I added.

"Carlton said Treblek's ex was surprised he came to the tavern for dinner." Sunny said. "She says they've been friendlier since their daughter disappeared, but the tavern isn't some place he frequents, even to eat dinner. He's a recovering alcoholic."

"Is she the night bartender at the tavern? What's her name?"

"Beatrice is her given name, but folks call her Bea," Sunny said. "She's worked as a bartender at the tavern for several years. I think she started there right after she divorced Treblek, so that must have been five or six years ago, maybe longer."

"How old was their daughter when she disappeared? Wasn't that about two years ago?" I asked.

"Pretty close to two years. Candace was the daughter's name. They called her Candy. I think she was nineteen."

"Have there been any updates on that investigation? Frank said Lieutenant Richardson was supposed to meet with Treblek tomorrow. Treblek told him he had some new information."

Sunny shook her head no. "Last I heard some other SLED guy had been handling the case. Nothing ever came of it. They suspected Candy's boyfriend at first, because they'd had a nasty break up shortly before she disappeared. Everyone thought Candy was cheating on him. However, the SLED guy said the boyfriend had a good alibi for the time she went missing. The kid was in jail. Investigators ran out of leads. No body complicated matters. Candy might have just run off with her new boyfriend. She wasn't getting along with her parents at the time either."

"Frank said Treblek was convinced Candy was dead."

"Yes, he was sure her body was in Swamp Lake. He tried for a year to get them to drain it. Crazy idea! There's no way Swamp Lake could have been drained, and the bottom is so muddy divers couldn't find anything at all."

"That's really sad not to know what happened to your child," I said.

"It would drive me crazy."

Sunny had a pained look on her face and then she groaned.

"Gracie, I think the baby is coming. I'm feeling a lot of pressure."

I called the nurse. Not long after that the doctor arrived. They confirmed the baby's head was crowning and the nurse prepared Sunny's stretcher for transport to the delivery room. Fortunately, Sunny's husband walked into the room before they wheeled Sunny out.

I excused myself and went to the waiting room. I decided I'd better call home to see what was going on there. I knew Max was still in Columbia, but our two youngest children had moved back home. This living arrangement was supposed to be temporary. Both of our kids had planned to find their own apartments; however John was working so many hours at the coffee shop and bakery that he had no time to look for a place, nor the inclination to do it. Lucy had planned to hunt for a condo closer to her office, but she started dating one of the Sheriff's deputies, so all her spare time was devoted to Deputy Steven Craig.

After I checked my watch, I realized it was too late to call John. He was probably asleep already, since he worked the early shift at the bakery. I called Lucy instead.

"Hey, Mom. Where are you?"

"I was going to ask you that. I'm at Beaufort hospital. Sunny's having her baby."

"Oh, that's great! Sunny said she was ready to get it over with."

"It probably won't be long now. I'm going to wait to be sure mother and baby are okay, then I'll head home."

"Did you get stuck out at Miller's Pond all afternoon or were you able to get back and finish your payroll?"

"I got the payroll done before I took Glenbrook and Samuelson out, but I did wind up helping them hunt for evidence. We were there until it started to get dark. I'm pretty sure the forensic team will be back searching the area tomorrow."

"So you didn't get a chance to push out those security updates?"

"No, I didn't even start on it."

"Do you want me to do it now? I'm planning to stay up late tonight. I'll be working the night shift all next week, so I need to get used to the change in routine."

"That would be great if you could at least start the updates, but I hate to ask you to do it. You worked all day. You should take it easy."

"I don't mind, Mom. I'd rather keep busy. Doing that will help me stay awake. Switching from day shift to night shift is a pain. I don't know how Steve manages it. He has to do it all the time."

"Well if you're sure you want to do it, you can go in my office there at home. I've got all my notes in the journal by my computer."

After we talked a couple more minutes, Lucy rang off to get started on the network updates. I stood in the waiting room trying to decide if I should get some food and coffee or just sit and wait. In the end I decided to stay put. I was afraid I'd miss seeing Coach if I left. It was a good thing I stayed. Coach came out after about a half hour. He was beaming.

"We have a little boy. Sunny and the baby are doing fine. Well, she's going to have a few stitches. Actually a lot of stitches. They should be in a room in a little while, but the nurse told me I had time for coffee."

"That sounds like a great idea. Let's see if the cafeteria is open," I said.

When we returned with our coffee, Sunny was in the room with her big little boy. He weighed in at ten pounds and was twenty one inches long, a healthy looking little fellow.

"Have you decided on a name?"

Sunny shook her head. "I wanted to call him Lashawn after his daddy, but Coach doesn't want to saddle the baby with being a Junior. It doesn't matter that everyone calls my husband Coach."

"You know I've called your husband Coach for so long I'm not sure I would have remembered his given name in a pinch."

"Lots of folks don't even know what it is. He's just Coach."

Coach just shook his head. "Okay, I know when I'm beat. If you want to name our little guy Lashawn go ahead. How about if his middle name is Anthony after your daddy?"

We chatted a little while longer then I said good night. I knew Sunny and Coach were both tired. I was too. I headed home.

When I walked in the kitchen, I found Lucy heating up some baked spaghetti. "Do you want some of this, Mom? There's plenty. Aunt Ellie sent home a shoo-fly pie for you too."

"That sounds great. I missed out on dinner. Lunch was a snack at my desk."

"I got all your security updates done. With all the hacking going on these days, I didn't want you to have to wait on those."

"I know what you mean. Sometimes it gives me nightmares thinking about all the spearphishing emails, Trojan attachments, and whatnot."

"I'm pretty paranoid about that too! But

tell me, did Sunny have a boy or girl?"

"She had a big boy. He was a ten-pounder. Cute as a button! I've got a picture on my phone. I sent a photo to Sunny's mom and to Carlton. I think they settled on the name Lashawn Anthony Collins. Did you know Coach's name is Lashawn?"

Lucy leaned in to see the photo of the baby. "He sure is cute. I like that name, but I sure didn't know Lashawn was Coach's real name. I don't believe I've ever heard anyone call him that."

"Sunny even refers to her husband as Coach. I wonder if the high school kids know his name."

Lucy fixed a couple salads while our baked spaghetti was heating up. When it was ready, Lucy and I sat down at the kitchen table and ate in companionable silence. When we started on our pie, Lucy began asking questions about Miller's Pond and the victim.

"I always thought the local hunters liked to keep Miller's Pond a secret, because they didn't want to share a good spot with just anyone," Lucy said.

"Miller's Pond is on private property. Old man Miller is very particular about who hunts there. He restricts the numbers, partly for safety sake, and partly because he doesn't like a lot of people tromping all over his property. I'm surprised he'd have Treblek there at dawn and then two more hunters later. Frank said those hunters found Treblek's body."

"Mom, you look tired. Your face is a little pink too. I think you got some sun this afternoon. Why don't I clean up the dishes and put the leftovers away. You head on to bed."

"It has been a long day and I'm not used to all that exercise. I've been spending way too much time sitting. I even missed some of my Tai Chi classes the last two weeks."

"Oh, I almost forgot. I stopped by the gym to check on the fall class schedule. Kevin Hobart is offering another self-defense class. When I signed up for it, he asked if you were going to take it again. How many times have you taken that class now, Mom? Three? Four?"

"I probably should take it again. I tend to get a little rusty without practice."

"Kevin said he thought he should let you teach the class at this point."

"Not on your life! I could take it a dozen more times and still not be ready to do that."

Chapter Three

Getting up the next morning was rough. I didn't make it out of bed until after eight, and that was only because a cat paw kept tapping my nose. Then the rest of the cat sat on my chest. Since Mibs is a twenty-pound Main Coon cat, he gets your attention fast.

When I finally did roll out of bed, I stumbled around the house until the caffeine from my first cup of coffee took effect. Besides suffering from lack of adequate sleep, I was stiff and sore from all the walking and standing. Two cups of coffee and a nice hot shower helped wake me sufficiently to function. The shower actually jarred me awake because it hurt my sunburned body. In addition to not being used to fresh air and exercise, my skin wasn't used to sunshine.

After I got dressed, I went into my computer room to check my servers. Pushing out updates sometimes means things don't work smoothly. This time everything seemed to be running well. No glitches had appeared, so I took a few minutes to check the Blue River Police Department evidence server to see if there was anything new posted about the murder. There was a note from the medical examiner with a preliminary time of death listed as approximately seven in the morning. He based his estimate on body temperature, lividity, and the fact that Rigor Mortis had begun. Using a metal detector the forensic team had found a bullet lodged in the dirt near where the body fell. The team also logged two shell casings, the plastic bag, cigarette butts, and feces, or scat, among other things.

As I was starting some research, Mr. Mibs jumped up on my desk and sat on my keyboard. He nudged the mouse in the process, so I watched my mouse pointer shoot around the screen and an odd combination of characters appear on the browser's search line. Mibs sat there glaring at me until I realized, in my morning stupor, I had forgotten to feed my two spoiled felines their half can of cat food. It didn't matter that they had a food dispenser full of dry food. Some things are sacrosanct. One must have one's Fancy Feast to start the day.

After I fed Mr. Mibs and Mrs. Peabody, I spent a few minutes researching scat and feces. Somewhere I had read they could find DNA in feces. I wondered if fecal DNA could be used to confirm a suspect's presence at a crime scene. That's if we found a suspect. Of course the pile of poop we found might have come from an animal, so that wouldn't help our case at all.

While I was pondering the situation, I received a phone call from my husband.

"Hey, Hon. How's it going?"

"Good. How's your class going?"

"Great! I think your brother is ready to head home though," Max said.

"Is it because he doesn't want to go to the banquet tonight?"

"Bud told me he would trade with you. He offered to do payroll for a year if you would drive over here and take his place at the banquet."

"I don't know why he has such an aversion to a tuxedo, or wearing any suit and tie for that matter. Ellie had to threaten him with his life to get him to dress up for Wylie's wedding."

"Did he have some kind of traumatic experience in a tux when he was little?" Max asked.

"Tell Bud he needs to buck up, and make sure you take photos of you two all dressed up. I want to put them in our family album."

"I will for sure," Max said. "Just a reminder, we're planning to stop at the farm on the way home tomorrow. I wanted to make sure that was still okay. Checking buildings and walking the fields will put us home early Sunday evening."

"That's fine. There's nothing going on here. Did they finally finish repairs on all the hurricane damage?" I asked.

"I sure hope so. I think they still have some fallen trees to clear but that's okay."

After we talked a few more minutes, Max had to end the call. His class was starting back up. I glanced through the evidence server again but didn't see anything interesting. I gathered my things to head to my job at the Bistro. There was probably a pile of invoices sitting on my desk and at least a hundred unread emails waiting for me.

When I arrived at the Bistro, I took time to duck next door for a latte. Making it through the day would require lots of caffeine. Ellie was busy with customers, so I made my own latte and went straight to my office to tackle the paperwork.

Several hours, numerous invoices, and seventy-five emails later, my sister-in-law stuck her head in the office. "Have you eaten lunch yet?"

"No, I didn't eat breakfast either."

"John is making sausage crepes. Interested in trying some?" Ellie asked.

"Yes, is it something new for the menu?"

"They're adding cream cheese and fruit stuffed crepes served with different syrups. John thought he'd try a savory recipe to see if that has possibilities. He's going to stuff the crepes with an egg and sausage mix, similar to a western omelette. Then he plans to cover them with sausage gravy. I thought that sounded pretty good."

"It does. I'll get a couple glasses of sweet tea and meet you at the family table."

I saved my work, organized my desk a little, and headed to the drink station to pour some sweet tea for us. Ellie and I arrived at the family table at the same time.

"My, that looks delicious," I said.

We were eating and chatting when my brother-in-law, Sheriff Frank, plopped down at the table. "What on earth are you eating?"

"It's stuffed crepes with sausage gravy. The crepes are stuffed with an egg mix," Ellie said.

"That sounds good. I'll have that and some tea. Carlton and I met with the mayor and county council. After that, I need something hearty. I hate politics! Sunny's lucky she's out on maternity leave."

I got up to fix Frank some tea, and Ellie went back to the kitchen to tell John he had another order for crepes.

When I returned with Frank's tea, I asked, "What happened at the meeting with the Mayor?

Can you tell me or is it top secret?"

"It's not a secret. The meeting was about the Fall Festival. They wanted to make sure we were coordinating our security efforts. And it wasn't actually the Mayor who was the problem. It is Mrs. Mayor and her harebrained ideas. Why on earth she thought a Fall Festival was a good idea I'll never know! We have the Arts and Crafts Bazaar in a few weeks. That's more fall-like than anything I've seen at this fiasco. She should have called it a Fall Carnival. It's all amusement rides and food trucks. There's no local presence and nothing resembling a celebration of fall and harvest time."

Before I could comment, we were joined by Maggie Wallace, owner of an antique shop down the street. Maggie is also President of the Blue River Art Guild. Ellie rejoined us too.

"Hey, Miss Maggie. Are you here to pick up an order?" Ellie asked.

"I didn't call one in. Thought I'd get some tea and visit a bit while I wait."

"I'll get your tea and a menu," I said.

When I returned with the menu and tea, I heard Frank continuing his rant on the Fall Festival. "Why does Mrs. Mayor think she needs a fund raiser? It's not for the Blue River Foundation, is it?"

"Yes, the profits are supposed to go to the foundation," Maggie said. "Honestly, I thought it was more for the Mayor's reelection campaign. She's setting up a booth at the festival. I'm not sure how that's going to work. I hope she opened things up for his opponents."

"For goodness sake, the election isn't for another year. Why do we have to think about election stuff right now?" Frank said.

"I know what you mean. It's bad enough we have to put up with it every four years," Maggie said.

"It's a royal pain!" Frank said.

"I'm surprised they opted to have the festival on the McKenzie property," I said.

"Park officials didn't want anything to do with that mess. After seeing what it looks like, I can understand why they nixed it. There wasn't any other location in the area big enough," Frank said.

"I'm really surprised local artisans and vendors weren't invited to attend," Maggie said.

"We were surprised she didn't ask the Bistro to set up a booth. Not that we minded. We've got plenty of catering jobs to keep us busy and we'll have a couple booths at the Arts and Crafts Bazaar," Ellie said. "I've got several wedding cake orders coming up too, so it's just as well."

"Another thing that's annoying is Mrs. Mayor had them open the festival grounds at noon today. You know some of the high school kids will cut out of school early to go to the festival," Frank said. "They'll be all over the place by this evening."

Maggie looked at Frank for a minute, then said, "I'm old Frank, but even I haven't forgot what it's like to be a teenager. Of course the kids will go to the festival. And if they didn't have the festival, they'd be finding another way to entertain themselves tonight. It's Friday."

"I heard Mrs. Mayor even persuaded the high school not to schedule a game tonight. She must have been working on this for some time.

High school game schedules are set months in advance. At any rate, we all thought that took a lot of … well, nerve, let's say," I added.

"I would have used another word myself," Frank said.

"Okay, Maggie, you came here to get food," I said. "I'll be your waitress today. What would you and Stan like? Today's lunch specials are Bistro barbecue on a kaiser bun with a side of loaded potato salad and fish tacos with Chef Rene's spicy red rice and slaw."

Maggie picked one of each and I went to the kitchen to deliver the order to chef and Bistro partner, Rosie Pratt.

"Okay, Miss Rosie, look at what I wrote down and tell me if I got it right?"

"One of each of the specials. Looks okay to me." Rosie laughed.

"How are you doing as chef? Do you miss the dining room?"

"I've actually enjoyed working the line this week, but I'd miss visiting with all our customers if I had to do this all the time. I see they got you doing waitress duty."

"Just for Maggie and Frank. This is Maggie's to-go order."

"Tell them hey for me. I'd like to visit, but Chef Rene is working on the catering order for our old friend, Malcom Dewey. You know we have to get it just right."

When I returned to the table, Ellie was getting ready to leave. She said, "I need to get to work. We're preparing some special desserts for a big catering order."

"That wouldn't be for Malcom Dewey, would it?" I asked.

"It would. If I don't see ya'll later, have a nice weekend," Ellie said as she scooted away.

"Don't tell me that pain in the neck has moved in already," Frank said.

"He didn't have much to move. Before he bought the Brodwin estate, he lived in that furnished cabin at the Irons' Estate, if you remember. He bought the Brodwin place fully furnished. Well, I think Celeste kept some special antiques and art work, but most everything else she left," Maggie said.

"Has Malcom contacted you, Maggie?" I asked.

Our conversation was interrupted when John brought out Frank's food order. That caused Maggie to ask about the dish and so our discussion was food related for awhile. Once John returned to the kitchen and Frank started eating, I repeated my question about Malcom.

"Oh, yes, he called me Monday," Maggie said. "Malcom asked about the Guild board. Someone must have told him we had two openings, since Celeste and Billie Jean are gone. He intimated that he could make a generous donation to the Guild Foundation and would consider a spot on the board."

Frank had a mouthful of food, but he managed to blurt out, "I'd be sure to get the money first before you agree to let old Dewey on your board."

"I agree with Frank on that score," I said.

"Malcom said something else that was interesting. I guess he met the gentleman who will be leasing the Newburg Estate. He said this Mr. Fitzpatrick might be a good candidate for our board. I've never heard of him, but Malcom suggested that he was well off and well connected."

"Maggie, hold that thought while I check on your food," I said.

When I returned with Maggie's to-go order, I asked, "You said this Mr. Fitzpatrick will be leasing the Newburg property. Does that mean the Newburgs aren't going to sell it?"

"Malcom said Fitzpatrick hopes to buy the property, but settling Jason Newburg's estate will take time, considering his widow is still under investigation," Maggie said.

"There are a lot of people who think Billie Jean was involved in Jason's death. If she's found guilty of being an accessory, she won't inherit anything. Someone, maybe the Mayor, told me Newburg's nephew likes their Blue River property and wouldn't mind keeping it," Frank said.

"Say, when are Max and Bud getting back? Are they having fun in Columbia?" Maggie said.

"They've enjoyed their certification course. It's given them a chance to reconnect with some old friends. I'm not sure how much they're going to enjoy the banquet tonight," I said.

Frank laughed. "Bud won't like it. That's for sure.

"I'm glad to see someone is finally acknowledging all the charitable work Max's mom did over the years. Too bad it's posthumously," Maggie said.

"I know. I wish Andy had come back to receive his mom's award," I said.

"Well, he's made a new life for himself in

Japan. Maybe he's better off there," Frank said.

Frank finished his meal and left for the Fall Festival. Maggie stayed a little longer, sipping her tea. We changed subjects and babbled about our children and grandchildren.

When Maggie left, I went back to work on invoices and emails. After that chore was finished, I updated our books. By supper time, my eyes were blurry and my brain was frazzled.

After my big lunch, I didn't feel like eating a heavy supper, so I made a small chef salad and poured an iced tea. When I got to the family table, I found my nephew Junior sitting there eating.

"Hey, Junior. They're actually giving you a chance to eat something other than fast food?"

"Yep. I'm killing time until the night crowd starts gathering at the Blue River Tavern. I'm supposed to talk to some of the regulars. Carlton wants me to see if anyone else remembers seeing Treblek on Wednesday. Carlton talked to some of the older folks last night, but he thought the younger ones might be more forthcoming if I asked the questions."

"Possibly. When do things get lively at the tavern?"

"On Friday and Saturday nights the crowd picks up when Elijah and his band start playing. They play their first set sometime after seven o'clock, I think."

"Maybe I'll just tag along with you. I haven't heard Elijah and Moses play in a long time."

About quarter till seven, Junior and I drove over to the Blue River Tavern. Their front parking lot was already filling up, so we circled around the back on the tavern's marsh side to find a couple empty parking spaces. When I got out of my suburban, I saw Elijah Moultry and the other members of his band unloading their instruments from their van. Junior entered the tavern, but I went over to say hello to Elijah and his cousin Moses.

"Hey Miss Gracie, I see you're wearin' your special deputy badge. That mean you be workin' tonight?" Elijah asked.

"I thought I'd talk to Vance Treblek's ex and maybe some of the regulars."

"Oh, yeah. We heard about Treblek. Sad thing. He sure was a mess these last couple years. Never did get over his girl's disappearance," Elijah said.

"You knew him?"

"He was a regular at the tavern until sometime after he and Miss Bea got divorced. He joined Alcoholics Anonymous I think. Sobered up and wouldn't set foot in the tavern after that. I was surprised to hear he came here the other night."

"You haven't spoken to him recently have you?"

"No ma'am, haven't talked to him in months. Toomey over there used to work for Treblek, you know." Elijah gestured toward a man holding a trombone. "Toomey operated a backhoe and some other heavy equipment for Old Treblek. That's until Treblek let his business go to pot and he started sellin' off all his machinery. Toomey, come over here and talk to Miss Gracie. Tell her about Treblek."

Toomey didn't look thrilled about talking to me, but he came over.

I smiled hoping to ease his anxiety. "I was just curious what happened to Treblek's business. Was it his drinking that was the problem?"

"Nah, he managed his business just fine when he was drinkin'. He'd stay sober all week. Good thing too, with the equipment we used. It was the weekends when he was out of control. After he joined that AA group, he did real good for awhile. Then his daughter disappeared; that's when his business went to hell. Oh, sorry Miss Gracie.

"Treblek just let the work slide. He'd take off for days. We could still finish a job without him, but it got to the point he wasn't schedulin' new jobs or he wouldn't follow up on a job. The other boys and I finally called it quits. We couldn't afford to lay about waitin' on him," Toomey said.

"Do you know what Treblek was doing when he took off?" I asked.

"Nah, not really. One of the guys thought he was goin' around to places where his daughter liked to hang out. We thought maybe he was followin' the girl's boyfriend at first. Treblek would drive over to Beaufort all the time. What else he was doin', I got no idea."

After several more questions, I felt I had held up Elijah and his fellow musicians long enough, so I let them pick up their instruments and head into the tavern. I brought up the rear.

Once inside, I took a minute to survey the scene. The tavern was divided into three main areas. There was the bar area with some small two-seat tables on the left. In the middle section, where the stage was located, there were larger four-top tables. The third section was an all-weather porch which faced out toward the marsh. Windows were opened on the porch and the ceiling fans whirled away.

Junior was sitting at one of the tables on the porch talking with a couple young men. I decided to head to the bar and talk to the bartender, Bea Treblek.

I sat down on a stool at the far end of the bar and waited until she came to take my order. When she finally came my way, her eyes focused on my badge and she scowled.

"I got to work here. I ain't got no time to talk."

"Fine, I'll have a sweet tea."

Elijah and his band started tuning up, so I turned toward the stage. Bea banged my glass of tea down on the counter and hustled to the other end of the bar. I decided to wait her out. I wasn't in any hurry and I enjoyed listening to Elijah and Moses play. I also did some people watching.

After fifteen minutes or so, Junior moved to another group of young people. While I watched him move across the room, I noticed another person in the tavern was watching Junior's movements with great interest. Junior only stayed with the new group about ten minutes and then moved to another table. All the while the man kept his eyes glued on Junior, I kept my eyes on that man. I also used my phone's camera to snap a photo of him. I tried to make it look like I was reading something on my phone, but I don't think it mattered. The guy was intent on watching Junior.

When Junior stood up to interview another group, that man got up and almost ran to the tavern's front entrance. I considered following him, but Bea got my attention.

"You want a refill on your tea, Honey?"

"Oh, yes. Thank you."

Bea picked up my glass and refilled it. When she set it down, it was more gently than the first time. I smiled while I paid her. I also added a generous tip to the amount.

"How come you're still working for the Sheriff's Department? I mean, you're old. You could retire and all," Bea said.

This wasn't the first time I'd been accused of being old for a police person. I was old, no denying that. I just smiled and nodded yes.

"This is just a part-time job. I did retire from my full-time job," I said.

"Well, if I could afford it, I'd be outta here for sure. I'm getting too old to work all night."

"It must be rough. Late hours and you're on your feet most of the night," I said.

"That's for sure. By the end of the night my back and feet are killin' me."

"Didn't you have part ownership in Vance's business? That should have brought you some money. I thought his excavating business was doing pretty well."

Bea shook her head violently. "Most of the money was tied up in equipment. I got some child support until Candy turned eighteen and a little alimony until Vance went all crazy."

"He went all crazy?"

"Yeah! He let the business go. Spent all his time tryin' to find out what happened to Candy. Don't get me wrong! I wanted to know what happened too. I've done a lot of cryin' and missed lots of sleep worryin' about our girl and what happened. It's just that he would take off for days. Didn't finish jobs or follow up on payments. Most all the guys that worked for him quit. Then Vance started sellin' off all his equipment. I think some of it might have been repossessed. He started to look bad too. Like he wasn't taking care of hisself. His eyes were kinda sunken. He had dark circles under his eyes. His skin didn't look right either. At first I thought he was drinkin' again, but he never smelled like booze or acted drunk. 'Course you can't always tell by that."

"So you and Vance never had any idea what could have happened to Candy?"

For a minute I thought Bea was going to walk away. I could see she had tears in her eyes. Then she finally said, "No idea! They thought maybe she got in a fight with her boyfriend. They broke up just before she disappeared. I never really thought that myself. Cory was a good kid. I think... well, I think he was the one who ended it with Candy. Not the other way around."

"Why did you think that?"

"Candy was actin' kinda funny. She dropped out of school. She had been takin' some college classes. She got fired from her job. She asked Vance and me for money all the time. We both told her she needed to either go back to school or get a job. I thought maybe she was drinkin' but she never smelled of booze. I wondered if maybe it was drugs. I just don't know. She wouldn't talk to me."

"Was she living with you when she disappeared?"

"She was. Before she broke up with Cory

she spent a lot of time at his place, so I'd go for days without seeing her much. I was workin' long hours myself."

By eleven o'clock Junior and I were pretty much done. We'd talked to quite a few customers. Most hadn't been in the tavern on the previous night. Of those who had been there, most hadn't paid any attention to Vance. I flagged Bea down to ask another question.

"Where did Vance sit the other night? He ate his dinner here right?"

"Oh, he sat here at the bar, near the middle of it. Why?"

"Who was sitting around him?"

"I don't know. I was real busy all night and I don't know every customer's name. I think Roger Stokes and his girlfriend, Sally, were sitting at the bar then. I don't remember anyone else."

Chapter Four

When I got home from Blue River Tavern, the first thing I did was make sure my cats had plenty of dry food and clean litter to avoid their ire. Then I went into the computer room to type up my notes on the night's interviews and upload them to the evidence server. After that I spent time searching for contact information for Candy's boyfriend, Cory Blackburn, and on Roger Stokes. Researching past records on Candy Treblek's disappearance seemed like the next step. Vance Treblek appeared to be obsessed with it. Sharing some new information with Lieutenant Richardson could be a prime motive for murder. Further research would have to wait. It was late and I was tired.

Saturday morning I woke up around seven thirty and decided I'd better spend time cleaning my house. I started by stripping our bed as soon as I rolled out of it, thinking that would spur me to action. After I showered, I wrestled clean sheets onto our king sized bed and then moved upstairs to John's room, stripping the bed and putting on clean sheets. When I got to the door to Lucy's room, it dawned on me that she might be in the bed since she was working the night shift, so I headed back downstairs for a cup of coffee.

Our calico cat, Mrs. Peabody, was sitting on the kitchen counter waiting for her half can of cat food. I scooped out the food onto two plates and put them in the utility room. I was surprised that Mibs wasn't there as well. He was the demanding one. However my body demanded coffee, so I went to our coffee maker and fixed myself a large latte.

As I sipped my coffee, I noticed Mibs was in the family room staring out the French doors. I went over to see what was so intriguing. Lucy was sitting on the deck. She had her cell phone in one hand and with the other hand she was feeding our neighbor's donkey, Jethro, a carrot. Beside her, waiting patiently for his treat, was our neighbor's Bullmastiff, Moose.

I grabbed a seat cushion and went out on the deck to join Lucy. We keep those cushions in our house because our neighbor's animals like to sit on our deck chairs too. The dog hair isn't too bad. It's the chickens and the goats that cause a mess.

Lucy clicked off her phone. I was pretty sure she had been talking to her boyfriend, Steve.

"Did you have another late night, Mom?"

"I went to the Blue River Tavern with Junior to interview some of the regular customers. Vance Treblek's ex-wife supplied some useful tidbits. So did one of Elijah Moultry's band members. Turns out the guy used to work for Treblek."

"It's a good thing you're helping. Practically all of Uncle Frank's deputies will be working the drug case."

"Drug case?"

"Yes, Steve told me they got a 911 call about two high school kids at the Fall Festival. The kids were frothing at the mouth. By the time the deputies arrived on the scene, the boys had passed out. Turns out the kids had overdosed. Blood work showed there was fentanyl and cocaine in their system. Both boys are currently in intensive care."

"That's too bad. I sure hope we don't have an epidemic of that kind of thing."

"I know. Uncle Frank plans to talk to the high school principal today to see if they can do some drug counseling on Monday. He's going to have his deputies talk to those boys' friends. I doubt they'll find out where the boys bought their drugs though. Steve expects several deputies will be in plain clothes at the Fall Festival to see if they can spot the drug dealer. I hope they find him or her soon."

"Me too. We sure don't want that stuff around here. That's really bad news. Say, have you had breakfast yet? I'm going to fix bacon and eggs."

"Sounds good. I'm too wired to sleep just yet. Working the night shift is awful."

I pulled some fruit out of the refrigerator to go with our bacon and eggs. When it was all ready, we sat at the kitchen table to eat.

"I was hoping Steve and I could have dinner tonight, but it looks like he'll be working late," Lucy said.

I started to comment when I heard my phone ringing. For a minute I couldn't remember where I'd thrown my purse. When I finally found it on the office floor, the call had ended. The caller ID showed it was Rosie. I figured I'd better call her back right away.

"Hey, Miss Gracie. Are you available to help out this morning?"

"Sure. What do you need me to do?"

"We need our produce order from Grub's greenhouse," Rosie said. "Elmer Grub is supposedly under the weather and Grub's boys say they can't leave the greenhouse. They say our order is boxed up and ready to go."

"Elmer is likely too drunk or too hung over to drive. He's probably not even at the farm. I'll bet he's in town, staying at his cousin's house. Bartenders take away his keys by the end of the night and he walks to his cousin Flint's place."

"That's a mighty long walk for an old man," Rosie said.

"He cuts through a section of Boardwalk Park, so it's not too bad. I guess I'd better get a move on if you need that produce."

"We're okay until supper prep. Then things might get hairy. We have another catering job."

"I'll get right on it."

I gobbled down my bacon and eggs but threw my fruit in a plastic container for later. Then I went to hunt sturdier shoes. My flip flops wouldn't work for driving.

The trip to the Grub's greenhouse was a pleasant one. The sky was a crisp blue with only wispy clouds here and there. It was the same route I had taken Thursday when I drove the Hardy Boys to Miller's Pond. The greenhouse was a few miles past Mill Pond Road. My route also took me past old man Miller's house. I was tempted to stop, but I figured I'd better pick up the produce first.

When I arrived at the greenhouse, the Grub brothers hustled out with the first of the boxes. I had to open the side doors as well as the back door on my Suburban to fit all the produce inside.

"You sure carry a lot of stuff in your Suburban, Miss Gracie. Is that a gun case?"

"Yes, it is. You'll probably have to put a box or two on the front passenger seat."

We managed to get all the boxes loaded, but it was touch and go. I had to do some creative stacking and rearranging to make it work.

Once I was back on the road, I decided I would stop at the Miller's farm house. There were one or two questions I wanted to ask Mr. Miller. When I pulled up at the house and got out, the front door opened and Mrs. Miller stepped out on the porch.

"Hey, Miss Ruthie. How are you?"

"Oh, I'm fine. I thought you were my boy drivin' up."

"I won't keep you. I just wanted to ask your husband a quick question."

"Harold ain't here. He's in the hospital. My boy's comin' to drive me there."

"My goodness! Is he going to be all right?"

"Yes, yes. They put in four stents. Had clogged arteries, you know."

"I'm sorry to hear that. I sure will keep you both in my prayers."

"Thank you, Miss Gracie. Can I help with something, since you drove all the way out here?"

"I wanted to check Mr. Miller's hunting schedule. I know he keeps track of everybody who's coming and when they're coming."

"Sure does. He writes it on the calendar on his desk. Here I'll show you."

We walked through the living room to the

bedroom they used as an office. Sure enough there was a calendar on the desk open to September. There were two names marked on the Thursday Vance Treblek was found dead and his name wasn't either one of them. His name was marked on the calendar on Monday and Tuesday of that week.

"Miss Ruthie, do you know if Vance Treblek was hunting on the property all week? I see his name for Monday and Tuesday, but not for Thursday."

"Oh, no, no. Vance was only scheduled for the two days. He only paid for the two days. Excuse me a second. I think I hear my boy. I'll tell him to wait a minute."

While Ruthie went to talk to her son, I used my phone to snap several shots of the calendar. Then I headed to the door so I wouldn't hold up Miss Ruthie and her son. I figured they were anxious to get to the hospital.

Once I got back to Blue River, I drove straight to the Bistro. I lucked out and found a parking place close to the rear entrance. Chef Octavio and a couple members of his kitchen crew helped unload the boxes of produce. When that was done, I went to my office and sent my calendar photos with a brief text explaining their significance to Carlton, Frank, and Lieutenant Richardson. They might know about the calendar already, but I wanted to be sure they had that information.

Carlton texted back, "Interesting! Thanks."

Richardson just texted, "Thanks."

I got a thumbs up from Frank.

I decided to take some time to read up on

Candy's disappearance. About one o'clock, Maggie Wallace stuck her head in the door. "Have you taken a lunch break yet?"

"No, I ate a late breakfast, but I'm ready for a break. Have you ordered yet?"

"Not yet. I thought if you'd join me I'd eat my food here."

"Okay, do you know what you want or should I get a menu?"

"I think I'll have the shrimp and grits special, lunch portion. Stan wants Bud's Bistro burger with your loaded potato salad and slaw."

"The shrimp and grits special sounds good to me too. Sweet tea to drink?"

"Yes indeed!"

Rosie was working in the kitchen again. I placed our food order and went to the drink station to pour our teas. When I got to the family table, I could tell Maggie was anxious to talk.

"What's up, Miss Maggie?"

"Malcom Dewey wants to invite the board members of both the Art Guild and the Irons' Estate to his house for cocktails. I'm not sure I'm ready for something like that. Clinton Musgrove wasn't too thrilled about the invitation either. He's not keen on having Malcom on the Irons' board."

"I don't suppose Malcom has mellowed any since he inherited the big bucks."

"Based on my two phone conversations with him, I'd say definitely not."

"Can you put him off for awhile? With all the work you'll be doing for the Arts and Crafts Bazaar the next couple weeks, you don't really have any spare time. Board members and volunteers won't have much spare time either," I said.

"That's a great idea. Clinton will go along with that. He's swamped too and he's always been such a help with the Bazaar."

"Speaking of helping, when you tell Malcom that you and the other board members will be too busy, you might ask him if he'd like to help with the Bazaar."

"Oh, you know he won't. When he taught painting at the Guild, he was always too busy to help with Bazaar prep work and he'd arrange to be out of town during the Bazaar weekend," Maggie said.

"I know," I said. "I'll bet he'll be too busy to help out with the prep work this time."

Maggie and I discussed the Bazaar until our food arrived.

"I'm not going to feel one bit guilty telling Malcom I'm too busy. Between working at the shop and all the Bazaar preparations, I haven't had much time for anything else. My house looks terrible. I even missed church and my book club last week. To make matters worse, my sister wants me to drive to Columbia to pick up some items she wants us to sell in the shop. She's moving into a condo and has to downsize," Maggie said.

"You can't put her off until after the Bazaar?" I asked.

"No, she's got a moving company scheduled to come the middle of this next week. As usual she didn't plan ahead. She doesn't want them moving the china and glassware she's selling. She's got some porcelain objects too. She offered to rent a trailer for the furniture she wants to sell. How am I supposed to haul a trailer with my little car?"

"Can Stan use his truck?"

"His truck is in the shop and Stan isn't in any shape to run all over the country. He's been having some health issues. With the medication he's taking, I don't think he should be driving. He's better off sticking to his regular routine, working on his refinishing and upholstery projects."

"I didn't know Stan was having problems. I'm sorry to hear that. Say, maybe I can help out. I've got a tow package on my Suburban."

"Oh, that would be nice, but you're so busy. I hate to impose on you."

"It's not an imposition. I actually have something I'd like to do while we're in Columbia. And I could visit with Paul and Mattie while we're there. I never miss a chance to see grandkids."

"If you're sure, could we go first thing on Monday. We should be back home late Tuesday."

"Let me call Paul and Mattie and make sure they're okay with having a house guest Monday night. I'd better let Max know my plans too."

Maggie's mood improved immediately. She planned to call Clinton Musgrove at the Irons' Estate first, so they could present a united front on the cocktail party issue. I would have loved hearing Malcom Dewey try to come up with excuses on why he couldn't help with the Guild Bazaar.

I had my own list of phone calls to make. My daughter-in-law said they were fine with a visit. My next call was to Max. He had been gone all week and I was looking forward to having him come home, but here I was making plans to take off for Columbia. Max, as usual, was very understanding.

"Maggie's probably right thinking Stan shouldn't be driving, especially trying to haul a trailer," Max said. "Paul, Mattie, and the girls will be happy to see you. They were disappointed you couldn't come with me this past week."

"Having Bud plus both of us absent would have been rough on the crew with the Bazaar coming up and all our catering jobs. I probably shouldn't be running around now, but Maggie is really stressed trying to juggle her regular work on top of the Bazaar. Besides that, I've got an interview I'd like to do in West Columbia."

"We'd better not tell Bud you're driving to Columbia. He still hasn't got over the tuxedo business. I did get some good photos of us at least."

Max and I talked a little longer and then he rang off to inspect some of the farm property. I still had a couple more phone calls to make. I called Detective Carlton Andrews first. He told me he was planning to come to the Bistro for dinner, so we could talk strategy then. My next call made me a little nervous, so I opted to text my intention to visit Columbia and talk to Candy Treblek's boyfriend, or rather ex-boyfriend, Cory Blackburn.

Lieutenant Richardson texted back, "Go for it!"

After that flurry of activity, I realized I'd better settle down to work. I had plenty to keep me busy, given that we had end of month and quarterly bookkeeping looming ahead of us. I worked steadily at my computer until supper time. Carlton texted that he had phoned in his dinner order to Rosie and was on his way. I saved my work, cleared my desk, and headed to the kitchen. Rosie was still working the line.

"You're still on duty, Miss Rosie?"

"I'm ready to quit. Just fixing dinner for me and Carlton. Do you want me to fix you something too? We've got some nice stuffed pork chops and baked sweet potatoes ready to go."

"That does sound good. How about if I get three salads and some tea?"

When we three gathered at the family table, we took time to enjoy our food before our conversation changed to recent crimes.

"Our prime focus is the search for the drug dealer," Carlton said. "We had another person overdose today. That person died. We'll all carry naloxone. That may save some lives if we have it available to treat overdose cases right away. We won't have to wait for paramedics to arrive. Frank's got his deputies carrying it now. He's got every available man watching the Fall Festival too."

"How come this has started all of a sudden? We've had some problems with drugs, but not this stuff loaded with fentanyl. At least I haven't heard of it here before now. Is it all because of the crowd coming for the Fall Festival?" Rosie asked.

"This latest victim doesn't appear to have been at the festival, but we don't have all the facts yet. This guy worked the second shift and got off at midnight. His girlfriend thought he was just tired and wanted to sleep. Stokes doesn't have any past history of drug abuse. I don't completely trust what his girlfriend says, but he's never had any contact with the law over it. There's nothing in his medical history to indicate he's had problems with drugs."

"Carlton, you say the latest victim's last name is Stokes?" I asked.

"Yes, Roger Stokes."

"There was a Roger Stokes sitting near Vance Treblek at the Blue River Tavern Wednesday evening. Could it be the same Roger Stokes, I wonder? His girlfriend's name was Sally."

"Sounds like it could be the same one. This guy's girlfriend is Sally Hopper. The two have been living together for a couple years. She works a half day on Saturday, so she didn't find him until she got home from work at two o'clock. He was gone by then," Carlton said.

"That's just sad," Rosie said. "I guess you're going to be pretty busy for the next several days."

"Afraid so," Carlton said. "We may have to talk to this Sally Hopper again. Tell me, Gracie, what's prompted you to talk to Candy Treblek's old boyfriend? You say he's living in Columbia now?"

"It's West Columbia. I wanted to ask him what kind of problems she was having when they broke up. Bea Treblek told me Candy dropped out of school and got fired from her job. Sounded to me like she might have been having drug or alcohol issues? Something was clearly going on with her. I can't find much on her background in our records. Since Maggie has to go to Columbia, I thought I'd help her out and see what I could find out from the ex boyfriend."

"The SLED person on the case has most of the background information," Carlton said. "From what Rich said, they took over the case right away. Frank wouldn't have been involved in that investigation. Candy and her boyfriend were living near Beaufort at the time."

"I was puzzled by Blackburn's current address," I said. "It looks like he's living near Cafe Strudel. Rosie, you remember our visits to Cafe Strudel in West Columbia?"

"I sure do. There's a row of shops along there. State Street right? We had a lot of fun visiting those shops and then lunching at Cafe Strudel. Does this Blackburn kid live in the apartments in that area? Aren't there some big apartment buildings nearby? There are some older homes around there, too. I forgot about those."

"Blackburn's address looks like it belongs to one of the shops on Meeting Street. I should have time to check it out while Maggie and her sister box up china and glassware. Maggie says she and her sister can load the trailer. I hope she's right. I'd like to have time to visit with Paul and Mattie."

"You don't mind hauling a trailer?" Carlton asked.

"No, I don't. It's not any worse than hauling our 22-foot bass boat. I've been stuck bringing that home and backing it into our garage many times. Say, Rosie, do you want to tag along and visit the shops? We could all do lunch at Cafe Strudel. You could stay with me at

Paul and Mattie's house. I'll bet they could be persuaded to play a hand or two of Whist after the kids go to bed."

"That's tempting, but I need to take Momma to the doctor on Monday. Otherwise I'd go."

After warnings to be careful in Columbia, Carlton returned to work. Rosie went home for some much needed rest, and I went home to finish cleaning my house so it wouldn't look like a pit when my husband returned from his travels.

On Sunday mornings my sister-in-law and I normally go to church together. We got in that habit because our husbands were almost always at work, either as paramedics or chefs. After church I dropped Ellie off at her house and then stopped at the grocery store before heading home.

Cooking isn't something I do very often, since there are so many chefs in the family and we spend so much time at the bistro. I do, however, have a couple meals that I can prepare fairly well. One of them is a crockpot roast. I prepped my roast and put it in the crockpot. Next I washed and chopped up the veggies so they would be ready to add later. After that I did laundry and cleaned the bathrooms. By the time Max got home the house was clean and supper was ready.

We had a nice quiet evening. Lucy and John joined us for supper. After we ate, I cleaned up the kitchen. Max was exhausted from tramping all over the farm, so we went to bed early.

Chapter Five

Monday morning Max was up early and anxious to get to the Bistro. He did, however, take time to fix a nice breakfast of French toast and sausage before he left. I cleaned up the kitchen, made sure the cats had dry food and clean litter, and then packed an overnight bag for my little field trip. By nine o'clock, I had picked up Maggie and the trailer and we were on the road to Columbia.

The trip itself went by quickly. The weather was perfect and traffic wasn't bad. We had plenty to talk about with the upcoming Bazaar, board meetings, and family. When we arrived on the outskirts of Columbia, Maggie directed me to her sister's house. I even managed to back the trailer into her sister's driveway on the first try. From there things went downhill rapidly.

Maggie's good mood plummeted as soon as her sister walked out of the front door to greet us wearing her bathrobe. When she started talking, I could tell that she and Maggie had very different personalities. Where Maggie was a planner and organized, her sister was... well, scattered. When we went into the house, we saw that she hadn't purchased any boxes as she had promised, and therefore, hadn't even begun to pack anything. I was afraid Maggie was going to explode.

Maggie's sister had the good sense to realize Maggie was upset. She assured us that she would dress right away and run out to buy boxes. I persuaded Maggie to join me for lunch, before she tackled boxing up china, glassware, and curios. I was afraid she might start throwing some of it at her sister. After unhitching the trailer, we beat a hasty retreat.

As we drove down Meeting Street, I asked Maggie to keep an eye out for Cory Blackburn's address. My plan was for us to eat at Cafe Strudel and let Maggie visit the shops on that street while I ran over to Blackburn's residence. When Maggie saw where he lived, she opted to join me. It was a bookstore. After driving around a bit, I found a parking spot on State Street. We walked back along State and crossed Meeting Street to the bookstore.

When we entered the building, we saw a small sitting area to our left. Behind that area were bookshelves. To our right was a long counter and behind that were more shelves. In front of us were rows and rows of shelves stretching from one end of the building to the other and reaching up to the ceiling. Scattered about were racks of DVDs, vinyl records, eight track tapes, video games, and even newspapers. We were looking at more of a book warehouse, a book collector's dream.

Maggie went off to browse the aisles and I approached the counter. There was a gray-haired gentleman sitting on a stool behind the counter squinting at a computer screen. He was obviously not Cory Blackburn, but I hoped he could help me find Cory.

The gentleman looked up when I reached the counter. "Good morning! How can I help you?"

"My name is Gracie Alderman. I'm trying to find Cory Blackburn. This was the address that was given to me. Does he live in this area?"

"My grandson lives over the shop. He's back in the stacks somewhere shelving books. He's not in trouble, is he?"

"No, no. I just wanted to talk to him a minute if that's okay."

"Sure. Sure. He's due to take a lunch break. Tell him to take his lunch break."

The gentleman went back to squinting at the computer screen and I went along the stacks looking for Cory Blackburn. I found him beside a rolling cart filled with books. When he saw me approach, he moved his cart closer to the shelves, so I could pass. Instead I stopped to talk.

"Cory Blackburn?"

Cory's initial smile changed to a frown. He looked at me for a minute. Then he gave me a hesitant, "Yes."

"My name is Gracie Alderman. I'm a Special Deputy for the Blue River Sheriff's Department." While saying that I showed Cory my badge. "I'd like to ask you a couple questions. Your grandfather said you could take your lunch break. You could eat while we talk. It shouldn't take long."

Cory led me to a door toward the rear of the building. It opened into a short hallway where there were a couple doors on either side, one of which was marked "Office." Another was marked "Restroom." Ahead of us was a break room. Cory motioned for me to sit down at the table. He walked over to the refrigerator, pulled a couple slices of pizza from a box in the frig, and slid the slices onto a plate. He put the plate in a microwave, put the box back in the frig, and retrieved a can of soda from it. He stood by the microwave, ignoring me, until it dinged. I knew he was stalling because he didn't want to talk to me, but I've learned that time is my friend. I wasn't in any hurry.

When he finally sat down across the table, he said, "You're here about Candy, aren't you? Have they finally found her?"

I thought that was a curious comment, but I proceeded. "No, they haven't found her, but I'd like to get some background information on Candy. I understand you broke up shortly before she disappeared. Can you tell me what led to your breakup?"

Cory just sat there for a couple minutes. He didn't make any effort to eat his pizza or drink his soda. He just stared at the table top. Then he finally said, "I really don't know what happened. She just changed. Like night and day changed.

"When we were in high school, we talked about getting jobs, renting an apartment together, and saving up for college. Well, I was the one who had to save for college. Candy could get college money from her folks. I thought things were going great. We both got jobs. I rented a small efficiency apartment near Beaufort and even managed to come up with enough money to take a couple classes. That's because my mom gave me a little of my dad's insurance money when I graduated. Candy stayed with me a lot, but she said her parents didn't approve of her living with me full time. I didn't complain. We were busy working and studying, so we only had a few days a week to be together. Even then we had to study. At least

I thought we were studying. Turns out she flunked out of school. Then I find out she lost her job. I found that out when she asked me for money. When I said I didn't have any to spare, she got mad. I tried to explain that I'd just fixed my car, but she wouldn't listen. She said I was boring and she didn't know why she ever wanted to go out with me. That hurt. I told her, 'If that's the way you feel, you can just take your stuff and get out.' It made me sick."

Cory took a swig of his soda. I gave him a minute, then asked, "Did Candy move out?"

"Not exactly. She stormed out of my apartment and drove off. I waited a couple days to give us time to cool down before I tried to talk to her. I tried texting her first. I asked her if she wanted to talk. At first she didn't respond. After about a week with me texting her every day, she texted back to leave her alone. Those aren't the words she used, but that's what she meant.

"A couple months passed. I didn't hear from Candy during that time. The lease on my apartment was up at the end of the month, so I decided to move here. Mom had already moved in with Grandpa. My granddad offered me a job. He said I could live free of charge over the shop. I figured that was a good deal. I could afford to take more classes and get my degree faster. I texted Candy that I was moving and told her to come get her stuff. She had some clothes at my place and a few odds and ends. I told her I needed her key back.

"By the end of the month, I hadn't heard from her. I texted her repeatedly to come get her stuff. I got to the point where I had to move out. I had my stuff boxed up and planned to clean the apartment and stay with a friend a couple nights until I could pick up my last paycheck.

"Well, my plans were changed. I got home from work early to find that Candy had been there. She had brought a suitcase, a small duffle bag, and a box for some junk she had, like candles, a music box, and stuff. It looked like she had shoved her clothes in the two bags, and then took off. I waited around to see if she'd come back. While I waited I cleaned up the place real good, so I could get my deposit back. I finally left to take my things to my friend's place. When I returned to the apartment, Candy still hadn't come back, so I put all her junk in my car, turned in my key, and went back to my friend's house. I texted Candy to call me. She never did.

"The next day I went to an ATM to get some cash and discovered that most of my money was gone. When I investigated, I found Candy had taken one of my checks. She wrote it out to herself and took my money. I was furious. I tried calling and texting her. She didn't respond. At that point I needed some cash real bad, so I decided to pawn her music box, her porcelain ginger jar lamp, and a couple of my things. That music box was a gift from me, so I sure didn't feel bad about it. The music box and the lamp together weren't even close to the value of what she stole from me, but I had to do something to get through until I got my last paycheck and my deposit check.

"The idea that Candy would steal from me, betray me like that… well, it just hurt that much more. I was really mad when I drove to the pawn shop. I didn't pay attention to the speed limit or stop signs. A cop pulled me over. I jerked my car over to the side of the road so fast the contents of the box dumped out. When the music box fell open, its content spilled out. Long story short, there was cocaine in the music box. They found some in the ginger jar lamp too. I got busted for possession and spent time in jail. I was a mess for a long time, I'll tell you. I couldn't think or talk straight I was so upset. I thought we loved each other. But no! Candy dumped me, stole from me, and then got me busted."

Cory paused for a minute to sip his soda. Those memories had obviously upset him all over again. He finally continued, "But, you know, my arrest turned out to be a blessing, because I was in jail when Candy disappeared. I think Candy's dad might have killed me otherwise. He was convinced someone killed his baby girl and I was his prime suspect."

"Did Vance continue to suspect you or did he change his mind?"

"He must have changed his mind. Not right away, you understand. It took time to convince him that I was incarcerated when she disappeared. You know, he even visited me when I was in jail. Asked me a bunch of questions."

"What questions did he ask you?"

"He wanted to know who Candy's friends were. Where she liked to hang out? I told him the names of our friends, but I told him we'd been too busy to socialize much. More like I'd been too busy. I don't know what Candy had been doing.

"The police, or maybe it was that SLED guy, asked me those same questions. I told him the same thing. I think they must have checked with our friends. They were mostly people we knew from high school. They hadn't had any contact with Candy for months either."

"Can you give me a time frame when things began to change?"

"Gosh, it seems like a hundred years ago now. I've tried not to think about that time."

"I can imagine it was rough. I'd really appreciate if you would try to remember."

Cory ate some of his pizza and took a sip of his soda. "I moved into my apartment the August after we graduated. Three years ago now. Hard to believe. My lease was up the following August. I don't remember the exact dates. Candy didn't even finish her first semester of classes. She got fired from her job sometime after the holidays. Maybe it was January or February. I'm not sure. She didn't tell me much. And I don't know how she was spending her time or what she was doing for money between that time and when she asked me for money."

"Did Candy's appearance change any? Did her speech change?"

"Well... I don't know. She started wearing more makeup I guess and dressing kinda ... well, slutty. Oh, I don't know. I'm telling you I've tried to forget all that. I've got my life here now. I'm doing good in school."

"I understand and I'm sorry I have to dredge up old, unpleasant memories."

"Say, if Candy hasn't been found, why are you asking all these questions?"

"Because her father was killed a few days ago."

Cory's mouth fell open and he just sat

there, not moving, staring blankly ahead. After several minutes, he swallowed. It looked like he was going to cry. "Oh, my God! Do they suspect me?"

His reaction would have convinced me that he was innocent, but I also knew that Rich had checked on Cory's whereabouts using a local parole officer. To calm him down I said, "You are not on their suspect list. Since Vance was so obsessed with his daughter's disappearance, I just wanted to get some additional background information. Do you think you could give me some of her friends' names? Is there anyone new she might have met after you graduated?"

Cory was still upset. He sat slumped in his chair for awhile. Then he said, "I guess I could give you some names."

I pulled out a small notebook and Cory started naming people. With the help of the contacts list on his cell phone, he was able to give me over a dozen names. He rattled off a couple names of people Candy had met through her job or school. Then he shook his head.

"I'm sorry. I can't remember anyone else. We didn't really hang with those folks much. I only went back to Beaufort once after I got out of jail. For awhile I didn't have a car. They sold the one I had when I went to prison. Mom moved here to live with Grandpa before I went to jail. She's can't really work full time, you know. She has to do dialysis."

"I'm sorry to hear that. You have a lot on your plate with your mom sick, school, and this job."

"Yeah, but it's okay. I like school. The

classes I'm taking now are real interesting. I kinda enjoy studying. Does that sound stupid? I like being around all these books. Mom says it's in my blood. She says we inherited it from Grandpa."

After a couple more questions, I gave Cory my business card in case he thought of anything else. I thanked him for his help and wished him well. He seemed like a nice kid. Then I went in search of Miss Maggie. She had commandeered a wingback chair in the sitting area by the front door and was reading a book. Beside her was a tote which appeared to be full of books.

"My goodness, Maggie, looks like you've been busy!"

"You need to get me out of here before I buy half the store. I'll be coming back for sure."

We retraced our steps to my Suburban to deposit Maggie's purchases and then headed to Cafe Strudel for lunch. Our timing was good. Around lunch time the place is normally crowded, but we arrived after the worst of the lunch crush was over. We got seated right away.

"What are you going to order?" Maggie asked.

"I'm leaning toward the green tomato BLT with their duck fat fries."

"That does sound good. I thought about getting their seafood mac and cheese. I'm torn."

After we ordered, we sipped our tea and spent some time discussing the art work on the walls. Then Maggie said, "I'm sorry I dragged you here to help me. I'm afraid it's going to take forever to get all Sis's stuff boxed and loaded. I can't believe she didn't get those boxes and get started."

"Well, she did say she had trouble finding boxes. Don't worry. I was glad to get a chance to talk to Cory Blackburn. His grandfather's store is certainly interesting. I'll have to visit it again myself."

"I know. It was great. But, tell me, did you find out anything new when you talked to Cory?"

"He told me things that were new to me. We didn't have much background information in our records. I guess SLED worked on Candy's disappearance from almost the beginning," I said.

"That Treblek case was sad. You know Candy came in our store and tried to pawn some things. That couldn't have been more than a month before she disappeared. I told her we didn't pawn stuff. Turned out the silverware she was trying to pawn belonged to her grandmother. I heard that from Rufus Freeman. You know Rufus, don't you?" Maggie asked.

"Yes, I know Rufus. He's always careful about what he takes for pawn or sale. He does a pretty thorough check to make sure it isn't stolen goods."

"He does," Maggie said. "Rufus actually called Candy's mom. I think he frequents the tavern, so he knew her. I guess Bea was really upset when she heard about the silverware. She said Candy didn't have permission to pawn or sell it. I don't know what happened after that."

Our food arrived, so we took time enjoying it. When we were done with the entree, we ordered coffee and opted to split a dessert. They had some luscious looking brownies.

"Let me get the check. You paid for gas to drive here," Maggie said.

While we waited for the check, my cell phone beeped. When I checked it, I saw that I had a text message from Cory Blackburn. It said, "Candy talked about a Sally. Don't know last name. Met her once maybe. Don't remember what she looks like either. Sorry."

I, in turn, texted Detective Carlton Andrews that piece of information, adding, "Thought you might want to ask Sally Hopper if she knew Candy Treblek."

By the time we arrived at Maggie's sister's house, Carlton had texted back, "I would love to ask Sally Hopper if she knew Candy. Unfortunately we can't find her. Sally seems to have disappeared."

Chapter Six

Stacks of boxes and piles of packing material greeted us when we entered Maggie's sister's living room. She had been busy in our absence. That was fortunate. We, in turn, got busy wrapping china and packing it in the boxes.

As we packed some glassware, I had to stop and look at one of the pieces. It was a cut glass serving dish that looked to be specially made for deviled eggs. I called to Maggie.

"Is your sister sure she wants to sell this? It looks like a really good piece."

"Oh, yes. She says all this stuff has to go. She doesn't have room for it and doesn't entertain like she used to," Maggie said.

"If she's sure she wants to sell this, I'd like to get it for Ellie's birthday. You know how much Ellie likes deviled eggs. She would love to have a fancy piece like this to serve them on."

"Gracie, if you want that piece you can have it. That's the least Sis can do, since you've helped so much."

"No, no, I'll buy it. It looks like a valuable piece."

After arguing back and forth for awhile, both Maggie and her sister insisted that the glass dish was my gift for helping. I gave up and took it out to my Suburban. Then I continued to pack with them until supper time when I excused myself to head over to Paul and Mattie's house. I'd promised to take the kids out to dinner and I was anxious to see my two granddaughters. The rest of the evening turned out to be very pleasant. I even got to read the girls their bedtime stories.

The next morning Paul chose to go into work late, so we had extra time to visit. After breakfast, I helped Mattie clean up. Then I packed up my overnight bag and headed back to Maggie's sister's. When I arrived I found that Maggie's nephew had begun filling the trailer with furniture. He used some bungee cords to keep it from shifting. It looked fairly secure. We loaded the rest of the furniture in the trailer and the boxes with breakables in my Suburban. Mid afternoon, after a fast food lunch, Maggie and I finally started home.

During our drive home Maggie didn't talk much. I think she was tired. She and her sister had stayed up late in order to finish packing. I turned on the radio and cruised down the highway to the mellow tones of Jon Batiste and his band, Stay Human. Their sound always reminds me of Elijah Moultry and his group.

The drive home wasn't bad, but when we arrived in Blue River, we had to unload all the boxes and furniture at Maggie's shop. Max and Bud were nice enough to come over to the shop and help out. I don't think Stan was in any shape to haul much furniture. Some of the boxes were heavy.

Max rode with me back to the rental place to turn in the trailer. By the time we finally got to our house, I was exhausted. While I ate a light supper, I took time to type and then upload my report on my conversation with Cory Blackburn to the evidence server. Once that was done, I was ready for bed.

The next morning Max left for the Bistro

early as usual. I rolled over and went back to sleep, waking up again around eight o'clock. I showered and dressed first thing.

My artificial knees were complaining about all the boxes and furniture I'd hauled, so I was moving at a snail's pace. I made some coffee and buttered a couple slices of raisin toast. Then I noticed that Max had made a pan of baked oatmeal. I went ahead and ate my toast, but planned to have the baked oatmeal for lunch or dessert later. Oatmeal, like grits, is good any time of the day.

After spending several days in the Bistro office and a couple days on the Columbia trip, I decided a day at home was in order. I started a load of laundry, grabbed another cup of coffee, and then went into my computer room to do more research. I wanted to find pictures of Candy Treblek and Sally Hopper for starters. After that, continuing the background searches might fill in blanks.

Secluded in my 'inner sanctum' of an office and immersed in my research, I didn't hear Lucy until she was right behind me. I jumped when she spoke.

"Sorry, Mom. Didn't mean to startle you. Who's that on your screen?"

"That's Sally Hopper. She's the girlfriend of one of the overdose victims. She may have known Candy Treblek too. Since we can't find Sally to ask her if she knew Candy, my plan is to send her photo to Candy's ex-boyfriend to see if he recognizes Sally."

"The department just put out a BOLO on a Sally Hopper," Lucy said.

"That's not a surprise. Sally and her

boyfriend sat next to Vance Treblek at the bar the night before he was killed. Vance wound up shot to death and her boyfriend is dead from an overdose. Your Uncle Frank always says to look for connections and he doesn't believe in coincidences."

"It does sound suspicious," Lucy said. "I'm going to get some breakfast and head to bed. I'm beat. It was a long night at the department. By the way we had another overdose case last night. The report came through that it was cocaine mixed with fentanyl in his system. I heard the kid had bad chest pains and was sweating heavily. He was hallucinating too. His parents thought he might be having a heart attack, so they ran him to the emergency room."

"That's too bad. I sure hope they find the drug dealer, or dealers. And soon!"

"You and me both. This stuff is bad news," Lucy said.

As Lucy turned to go into the kitchen, I said, "Your dad made a pan of baked oatmeal if you want that for breakfast."

"Oh, that's sounds good!"

Lucy went to the kitchen to get breakfast and I went back to my research. Since there still wasn't much in the way of background information for either woman on our server beside my input, I continue my own background checks. I worked steadily until three o'clock when Max called.

"Can you come over to the Bistro for an early supper?" he asked.

"I guess so. I lost track of the time. What's going on?

"We're going to have a quick Bistro Group partners' meeting. It shouldn't take too long. Rene and Clinton have an idea they'd like to float to us."

"Okay. I can be there. How's you're day going?"

"Not bad. Bud and I have to go over to the fire department for a meeting tonight. The Chief wants to make sure everyone is up to speed on the drug situation and has a supply of NARCAN. We're going to be training police officers and deputies about how NARCAN works, so they know what to do when the NARCAN wears off. They need to understand that overdose victims need to get further medical treatment. This training is a good thing, believe me. Frank was here for lunch and said they had another overdose case. We've got a real problem."

"Lucy told me about that. It was another high school kid," I said.

"Bud and I may have to work the paramedic booth at the Arts and Crafts Bazaar. The Chief is worried about having enough coverage with the way things are going."

"If you two have to do that, we'll figure a way to manage. I plan to help Ellie with her bakery booth. Rosie's already lined up a bunch of our college kids to work the Bazaar."

After talking a few more minutes, Max rang off and I went to put on some more presentable clothes and a little makeup before heading to the Bistro. Somehow faded blue jeans and an old t-shirt just didn't seem right for a partners' meeting.

When I arrived at the Bistro, some of the

partners were already assembled at the family table. I grabbed some sweet tea from the drink station and joined Ivan and Ellie.

"Ivan, it seems like ages since I've seen you. How's your mom doing?"

"She's managing. It's not too hard on her now that the kids are older. Would you believe they're even helping her with the house work? Never thought I'd see the day."

"I miss seeing Gavon and Davona here at the Bistro. I used to enjoy their after-school visits."

"They miss visiting here. I don't think they find the Italian Bistro as interesting as this place."

The arrival of Chef Rene and Clinton Musgrove sidetracked our conversation. Then Bud, Rosie, and Max brought out our dinner, oyster po' boy sandwiches with sweet potato fries.

"There goes my diet! I was hoping to take off a few pounds," Ellie said. "You're not helping."

"I know. Those sandwiches are huge," I added. "They're big enough for two meals."

"Okay, let's get this meeting underway. Max and I have a meeting at the fire department tonight, so if we're going to have some lengthy discussions, we'd better get the show on the road," Bud said.

"What about Octavio? Is he coming?" I asked.

"He's going to listen over the phone. I'm calling him now," Max said.

After Octavio was connected, Rene started his pitch.

"Most of the guests at the Irons' Estate spend half a day touring the museum and the manor house. With the addition of the gardens and the soon-to-open Brodwin greenhouse, guests could be spending the better part of a day there. We thought a tea shop might be a good idea. That way guests could have lunch or afternoon tea without leaving the property," Rene said.

"That makes sense. Are we going to be involved in the tea shop?" Ivan asked.

"We thought it would be smart to lease the shop to the Bistro Group," Clinton said. "You folks know how to run a restaurant and have your business resources already in place. I was hoping Rene would be the chef, but he wouldn't have time to do it all."

"Where do you plan to put the tea shop?" Ellie asked.

"We thought about expanding the porch off the kitchen. Rene thinks our newly remodeled kitchen will be more than adequate for the job," Clinton said.

"It worked real well for Wylie's reception," Ellie said.

"What kind of time frame are we talking about?" Max asked.

"I guess that depends on what y'all think about this," Clinton said.

Rene pulled out a folder with artist's sketches of the proposed structure, an architect's floor plan of the first floor of the Irons' mansion with tea shop addition, and a sheet with a cost estimate. We took time to study them and eat our sandwiches.

"Rene, if you'll be spending your time at

the tea shop, does this mean we'd need to hire another chef or two?" Ivan asked.

"Probably so."

Rosie spoke up. "I think having a tea shop makes sense. People visiting the estate don't want to drive back to town for lunch and then turn around and drive all the way back to the estate. That's just too much driving."

"I like the idea too. It also makes sense that we handle the business end of the tea shop. That would free Rene up to concentrate on food," Ellie said.

"That all sounds good to me," Bud said.

Rosie looked at Max. "Well, Max, what do you think?"

"I knew about this beforehand. Clinton asked the charitable trust for funds to build the tea shop. I thought it sounded like a good idea. Having the Bistro Group manage the tea shop also sounds good."

Even Chef Octavio, who usually remains fairly quiet at our meetings, seemed to be enthusiastic about this new project. After another half hour or so of discussion, it was decided that the Bistro Group would manage the Irons' tea shop and we set out the next steps, talking to lawyers being number one.

After our meeting and our meals were finished, we all helped clean up the table. Max and Bud headed over to the fire station and I went into the coffee shop with Rosie and Ellie for an after-dinner latte and chat.

The coffee shop still had several customers occupying tables and in the sitting area on one side of the front door. However there were seats on the other side, so we got our coffees and sat down.

"I should've got a decaf. I'm supposed to work the early shift tomorrow," Rosie said. "Oh, well. I'll probably wait up for Carlton anyway, so it won't make a difference."

"Has he been working late hours?" Ellie asked.

"He sure has."

"This drug overdose business has got them all working extra long hours," I said.

"I hope we don't have any drug problems at the Bazaar. Poor Maggie doesn't need more things to worry her at this point," Rosie said.

"She's always stressed over the Bazaar, but I think Stan's health issues have caused her extra anxiety. She just about lost it in Columbia. Her sister hadn't even purchased boxes, let alone started packing. Maggie was fit to be tied," I said.

"Doggone it! I was going to bring up something at the meeting, but I got sidetracked by the tea shop business. It's actually something that Frank suggested," Rosie said.

"What's that?" I asked.

"Frank said he'd heard some town was considering using food trucks for surveillance at big events. He wondered if the sheriff's department could persuade the Bistro to buy a food truck. At first I thought he was joking but after we talked awhile, I got the idea he was serious," Rosie said.

"I wouldn't mind having a food truck." Ellie said. "It sure would be easier than setting up tents. The Guild Bazaar isn't too bad, since we can use the Guild kitchen and refrigerator, but other events are a real pain. And tearing things down is almost worse than setting things up."

"I agree with that. I wonder if we could persuade Max and the charitable trust to fund or maybe partially fund a surveillance food truck," I said.

"I'm all for asking him. Want to do it tomorrow?" Rosie said.

"Do you think it's too much to take on at once? We'll be doing the tea shop now," Ellie said.

"The tea shop will take time, since they have to build the addition. And the idea will have to be presented to the board first. We could do the truck rather quickly, I think. Especially if Max will help fund it," I said.

"So we talk to him tomorrow morning?" Rosie asked.

"I was planning to go to Beaufort tomorrow morning, but I can go there in the afternoon," I said. "We can talk to Max in the morning."

"Are you going to visit your mom?" Rosie asked.

"I probably should. It's been awhile. I'd actually planned to check out the place where Candy Treblek used to work. It's Bitsy's Shop. I think it's close to Mavis and Mo's place."

"It is. It's a neat place. They have some interesting gift items. Expensive stuff," Rosie said.

"If you're going to be close to Mavis and Mo's, could you pick up some coffee?" Ellie asked.

"Sure. And if I'm going to visit my mother, I'd better take one of your pies to her."

"You'd better have Bud fix up a cooler of food to take too," Ellie said.

"Wait a minute. Tomorrow is payroll day. I can't take off like that. I'll have to wait until Friday to go to Beaufort. Ellie, can you wait on your coffee for another day?" I asked.

"I can. We could postpone talking to Max until Friday if that helps," Ellie said.

"Yes, there's no rush on that," Rosie added.

"No, let's talk to Max tomorrow morning. I can spend the rest of the day on payroll. Postponing Beaufort until Friday is the best idea. I won't need to rush and paying a quick visit to my mother is almost impossible. That will give me time to visit with Mavis and Mo too."

After mentioning the bookkeeping that had to be done, I decided to spend a couple hours working in the Bistro office. When Max texted that he was done with his meeting at the fire station and was heading home, I saved my work, straightened my desk, and headed that way too.

The next day was busy. I got to the Bistro early to get started on payroll. Mid morning, Rosie, Ellie, and I went upstairs to Max's office to discuss the surveillance food truck. At first Max laughed when he heard the idea, but then he got serious.

"Having a truck would be good for the Bistro," Max said. Let me look into what's available and the cost. I'd better talk to brother Frank to see if he's serious about using a food truck for surveillance. If he is, I wonder if he expects us to train deputies in the art of cooking and food service."

"Lucy would appreciate it if you would train one particular deputy in the art of cooking," I said.

After we left Max's office, I went downstairs to my hole-in-the-wall. Rosie followed me.

"I can't believe Max jumped on the food truck idea so quickly," Rosie said.

"Well, he's going to look into the cost. The charitable trust can afford it."

"I know, but the trust is helping to build the tea shop."

"The trust can afford to do that too. Max's mom wanted to help the community and anything that involved the art community was a priority for her."

With that settled, I spent the rest of the day on payroll and bookkeeping, taking only a brief break to grab some lunch. By the end of the day, I was sick of invoices and emails. I also had a scary thought when I realized that, with a tea shop and a food truck in the works, there might be even more invoices and emails coming my way.

The next morning I woke up refreshed. I was looking forward to the drive to Beaufort. After showering and dressing, I decided to check on the evidence server. It was then that I realized I had forgotten to send Cory Blackburn the photo of Sally Hopper. Was that a senior moment? Maybe I had too much on my plate. Whatever the case, I sent Cory a text with the photo attached, asking if he recognized her.

By the time I picked up a cooler full of food and a pie to take to my mother, I still hadn't heard from Cory. He probably didn't want to think about that time in his life. I decided to wait before I called him. I didn't want to scare him off.

When I arrived in Beaufort, I went straight to Bitsy's Shop. The clerk on duty was less than helpful. She informed me that she was new and that I'd have to talk to the owner, Bitsy, who should be returning to the shop about one o'clock. I left the shop and walked down the street to Beaufort Coffee Roasters to visit with my friends, Mavis and Mo.

"Miss Gracie, what a pleasant surprise!"

"Hey, Miss Mavis. I had some business in town so I thought I'd stop by to visit. Of course when Ellie heard I was coming here, she asked me to pick up some coffee."

"Naturally. How about if I fix us some lattes and Mo can work on getting your order ready."

"A latte sounds great."

When we sat down with our coffee, Mavis said, "Look at my face. Notice anything odd?"

I looked at Mavis' face. She had the same caramel colored skin as our Rosie and she didn't have wrinkles like I did. Her hair was a salt and pepper. I knew she was wearing a wig, because her hair had not grown back completely after the chemo therapy. Still she looked great. Her face had a warm glow. Her eyes sparkled.

"I think you look beautiful, Mavis. I don't see anything odd at all."

"My eyebrows and eye lashes. Do they look wonky to you?" Mavis asked.

I looked at her again. "No, not at all. What's the problem with them?"

"I realized this morning that the reason

I'm having trouble putting on my eye liner is that I ran my brush along my eye lashes. I don't have any lashes yet. My eyes are still puffy. That's why my eye liner hasn't been going on smoothly. My hands are still shaky too. And look at my eyebrows! I don't have much of any hair there either. I hardly know where to run my eyebrow pencil. I look crazy!"

"No you don't, Mavis! I didn't notice either shaky eye liner or crooked brows. You look just fine. Really!"

"You're not just saying that to make me feel good?"

"No! And I was a little jealous that you don't have any wrinkles. I think you look great."

Mo had overheard our conversation and I saw him shake his head. He said, "I've tried to tell her she looks fine, but she won't believe me either."

Mavis raised her penciled eye brows. "Oh, Mo, you have to say that. You're my husband."

Visiting with Mavis is always a treat, but after more than an hour of gabbing, I figured I had kept Mavis from her work long enough, so I said good bye and headed to my mother's house. My mother insisted on feeding me lunch and we spent time catching up on the latest gossip. I had to insist that I had work to do in order to get away.

When I got back to Bitsy's Shop, I took a minute to check out the merchandise. It was definitely more high end household décor and gifts. The clerk from the morning had been replaced by an older, well-dressed woman. I didn't think she was as old as me, but her hair was completely gray. She was wearing a bright crimson suit and looked very sophisticated. I pulled out my badge and approached the counter.

The woman looked up from her notepad and smiled. "Can I help you?"

I showed her my badge and said, "Are you by chance Bitsy?"

The woman frowned but nodded yes.

"I'd like to ask you a couple questions about a former employee, Candy Treblek."

"Goodness, it's been years since she worked here. The SLED folks asked me a bunch of questions after she disappeared. Why are you asking questions now? Have they found her?"

"No, they haven't found her. We have a new case and information about Candy might be relevant to that case."

Bitsy looked skeptical but shrugged, "I'll do my best to remember. It's been so long. What do you want to know?"

"How long did Candy work for you?"

"She started here right after she graduated from high school. She seemed like a nice kid, well spoken and all. She dressed nicely. For awhile she did well. Then after Christmas that year I noticed some problems. It was when I was doing inventory for taxes. The money and the inventory didn't match."

"What happened? Do you think she stole from you?"

"I know she did. I had a couple security cameras installed around the counter area. She pocketed some of the money from cash sales. I confronted her. She tried to deny it, but I showed her the video. I told her she could pay me back or I would call the police and her parents."

"How much money did she steal? Did she pay you back?"

"I was short about five hundred dollars. She paid back some of the money."

"After you gave her the ultimatum about paying back the money, how long did it take her to pay you back?"

"Only a week. She came into the shop one day and gave me a fistful of cash. It was three hundred and fifty dollars. She told me that she'd pay me the rest later. I honestly was surprised that she paid me anything and not at all surprised when she didn't return to pay back the rest of the money. Her father actually paid me the rest of it, so I wouldn't call the cops."

"How did Candy look when she came to pay you? Had her appearance changed any?"

"Oh, I don't know. It's been so long ago. She was wearing more makeup. I remember that."

"So Candy worked for you from July to December? Or was it January? Did you notice any problems before you discovered the theft of the cash?"

"Well, at first she was very punctual and didn't miss any work. I tried to schedule her work hours around her class schedule. Toward the end of the year, close to Christmas, she called in sick several times and started showing up late. That's a bad time of year to have unreliable employees. That's when I do my best business. She started out as such a good worker and then she changed. I understand she dropped out of school too."

"Yes, she did. Did you have any other employees at the time? Do you know any of her friends?

Bitsy looked startled. "Why yes. Sally."

"Sally Hopper?"

"Yes, Sally has been with me for four years. Well, until just recently. She up and quit this past Sunday."

Chapter Seven

Bitsy had no idea what prompted Sally Hopper to quit. She said Sally was supposed to work the previous Sunday. Instead Sally picked up her paycheck Sunday and walked out.

As soon as I got out to my Suburban I called Carlton.

"That's interesting," Carlton said. "We didn't know Sally worked at Bitsy's. She told us she worked as a waitress. We checked on that. She must have been working two jobs."

"That's not unusual. I know a lot of folks who need to work two jobs to make ends meet. Actually, I know a lot of folks who work three jobs."

"Well, if she worked at the same place Candy worked, that sure is a connection as Frank would say. I'll update Rich when I see him later."

After my conversation with Carlton, I headed back to Blue River. I stopped at the Bistro's coffee shop long enough to unload Ellie's coffee and headed home to type up my report from my interview with Bitsy. As soon as I finished, I hit the recliner and listened to a security pod cast, "Security Now" with Steve Gibson. I was worn out and the podcast was my compromise between working and resting.

Saturday proved to be a relaxing day. I spent the morning paying bills and shopping online. For one thing, I wanted to order some bejeweled eggs from a local craftsman to add to Ellie's crystal deviled egg dish. Max worked the morning shift at the Bistro. When he got off work, he suggested that we drive to the park and walk the trails. It had been awhile since we'd done anything like that, so it was a real treat. During our stroll along the trails, we didn't think about work, drug problems, or anything other than the nature around us and the glorious fall weather. When we got home, Max heated up some leftovers and we had a quiet dinner while watching television.

"I'm glad we went to the park this afternoon. That was nice," I said.

"I know. It felt good to get out like that. I figured we'd better take advantage of the day. This next week is going to be hectic with bazaar prep on top of everything else."

"You're right. Everything seems to take a backseat to bazaar prep."

And everything else did. Well, except the normal work at the restaurants and coffee shop. They were business as usual. Everything else was crazy. I was roped into baking cookies and cupcakes. The bakery crew had to be desperate for help if Ellie had me working in the kitchen.

I had so many bazaar-related tasks to do that I didn't even think about police investigations. One of my major jobs was keeping poor Maggie from having a heart attack. It took us several hours to map out where to place each of the vendor tents. We had more entries than in previous years and past layouts didn't work. For Maggie and me there didn't seem to be enough hours in the day to deal with anything other than the upcoming bazaar.

Thursday evening the Bistro crew set up two tents in the patio area on the side of the Guild building. That gave us easy access to the

Guild kitchen and electricity, two very important requirements for our business.

Friday, long before dawn, Bud and Ellie drove the Bistro's catering truck, loaded down with supplies, to the Guild. Max and I followed in my Suburban with more supplies. We were met by Rosie and her first shift of helpers. By eight o'clock we were serving our first round of customers, the other vendors at the bazaar.

By ten o'clock the crowd started to get heavy. I was busy working the espresso machine, so I didn't have any chance to tour the bazaar. Things were so crazy Lucy offered to take photos of the booths and the crowds for the Art Guild website, normally my job. She even uploaded the photos.

We lucked out on another point. Bud and Max were able to take turns at the paramedic booth, so at least one of them was free to help Rosie with the Bistro's food booth. It was a good thing they were. Bazaar attendees seemed to be as interested in food and drink as they were arts and crafts.

We started the morning with a variety of breakfast sandwiches and pastries. John's sausage crepes were a hit, as were grits with cheese and bacon. Around eleven we transitioned to a lunch menu and desserts. Our friend Imogene delivered her moonshine chocolate truffles and bourbon balls before noon. They were sold out by supper time. I texted her to bring larger batches Saturday and Sunday.

Around three o'clock my feet and back were beginning to hurt. Ellie was limping and her face showed quite a bit of pain.

"Ellie, would you like to take a break and

get off your feet for awhile? Since Jacob is here now, we should be okay."

"How about you? How are you doing?"

"I'm regretting not working out at Hobart's Gym this last month. I think the only exercise I've had lately has been walking around Miller's Pond and loading and unloading furniture and boxes."

"The guys manage to get to the gym regularly. Why can't we do that?" Ellie asked.

"Other things seem to get in our way. You go take a break. I'll take one when you get back. Go put your feet up. Take my keys and relax in the Suburban," I said. "And get some real food. All you've had are coffee and donuts."

After Ellie took off, I had a rush of customers wanting espresso drinks. We managed. Jacob Moultry was a big help. He had mastered all aspects of our food service business, so he was able to jump in to help just about anywhere. I had a passing thought that I should teach him how to do payroll. That was only a passing thought, because we had a line of folks ordering mochas, lattes, and the dreaded frappes. I say dreaded, because they are a sticky mess to make when you're working outdoors, and our blender power cord seemed to get unplugged all the time.

I turned from the espresso machine to deliver a couple of drinks to a waiting customer when I noticed Jacob was taking an order from Malcom Dewey. He noticed me too, so I had to say hello.

"Why Mrs. Alderman, I had no idea you would be working here."

"We've had a booth at the bazaar every

year since the Guild started having them."

Malcom's face registered the slightest bit of annoyance. I attributed that to the fact that Malcom had never attended a Guild bazaar before. He stood up a little straighter.

"Well, it's nice that the Bistro folks support the bazaar. But where are my manners? Gracie Alderman, I'd like you to meet Herbert Fitzpatrick. He hopes to move to Blue River and I thought I'd show him the sights. He might even be persuaded to join the Guild board. I know he will be a great asset to the Guild and the community.

"Herb, Gracie Alderman is on the boards of both the Guild and the Irons' Estate. Her family members are partners in the Baker Street Bistro. They also own the Italian Bistro over by the interstate."

Mr. Fitzpatrick smiled. We shook hands.

"It's nice to meet you, Mr. Fitzpatrick."

"Please call me Herb."

"Then you have to call me Gracie. What drinks are you having?"

Malcom stiffened. "Just plain black coffee for me, thanks."

I looked at Herb. He said, "I'd like a large cappuccino, please."

"Certainly."

When I handed the gentlemen their drinks, Herb said, "This bazaar is really quite impressive. I don't believe I've seen such a diverse selection of arts and crafts. The quality is amazing. I had heard that Blue River was a mecca for artists and craftsmen, but I didn't realize just how true that was."

"We are quite proud of our artistic

community. Have you had a chance to visit the Irons' Estate? Jeremy Irons was the one responsible for luring artists here to Blue River," I said.

"So I've heard. I'm hoping Malcom will take me out to the estate soon," Herb said.

"Of course! Of course!" Malcom said. "It's been nice visiting with you Mrs. Alderman, but we really need to push on if we're going to see the rest of the booths before the end of the day. We've been invited to the Mayor's cocktail party tonight. We certainly don't want to be late for that."

Malcom and Herb walked away and we had another rush of customers. By the time Ellie returned from her break, I was more than ready to take mine. I grabbed one of my brother Bud's barbecue sandwiches and a soda and headed to the Suburban to put my feet up.

While I ate, I scrolled through my phone to see if I'd received any interesting texts and emails. Nothing grabbed my attention so I decided to play some games. My brain needed a diversion. While I was engrossed in a Sudoku game, someone knocked on my car window and startled me.

"Carlton, my goodness. Have you been patrolling the bazaar?"

"Yes, but I'm taking a break to eat. I've been walking around the booths and grounds for hours. All the picnic tables are full so Max told me to sit in your Suburban. Rosie said your Suburban seats were more like sofa seats so that sold me."

"They are. This has become our official break room. Climb aboard. You sit on this side.

I'll move around to the driver's side."

After we got settled, I gave Carlton a chance to eat some lunch before hounding him with all my questions. When he finished his sandwich, I couldn't wait any longer.

"So what's the scoop on the drug situation?"

"Not much so far. Just more bad news. Another overdose victim died. The first two high school kids are still in intensive care. We've got no leads from our interviews with their friends and Sally Hopper seems to have vanished off the face of the earth. Frank put a BOLO out on her car, but we've had no sightings. This is not good!"

"Has Rich made any progress on the Treblek case?"

"Rich and his guys have been helping us with the drug investigation the last couple days, so no. We could use another half dozen or more people to help us, but we're going to be short one instead. Junior got word that he passed his tests and the background check, so he's submitted his FD-140, the official application for employment to the FBI," Carlton said.

"That's great! Junior has wanted this for a long time."

Carlton nodded and pointed to something outside my Suburban. I turned to see my brother-in-law ambling up to my vehicle. I rolled down the window.

"Hey, Frank, want to rest your feet?" I asked.

"I'd like to do more than rest my feet, but unfortunately duty calls. I was looking for Carlton. Max told me he was here."

Carlton laughed. "Max told me to eat in their break room. Much more comfortable than those picnic tables, got to say. What's going on?"

"The DEA guys will be here at four. I told them to meet us at your office. Rich will join us there."

"So the DEA is getting involved?" I asked.

"Yep, they've been tracking this stuff as it's progressed from state to state. I guess this junk has a special chemical signature. Anyway they want to find the dealers' big boss pretty bad," Frank said.

"Don't we all," Carlton said.

"For goodness sake, don't let Sunny know about your meeting. She'll take herself off maternity leave and be down at the station even if she has to bring her baby boy with her," I said.

"Don't worry. I had a devil of a time trying to not discuss the investigations last night when Rosie and I took baby clothes to her," Carlton said. "If it weren't for Rosie and Sunny's mom distracting Sunny with baby talk, I'd have been in big trouble. Sunny was upset enough at the prospect of losing Junior to the FBI. I regretted telling her that, believe me!"

"I didn't realize the background check was completed. I thought maybe I'd be interviewed," I said. "I'm a little disappointed they didn't talk to me."

"You should be happy. Special Agent Wilcox's idea of an interview was similar to being grilled by Gator Joe or your favorite Lieutenant. On a scale of one to waterboarding, it made waterboarding look like fun and games," Frank said.

"I've got to agree with that. Wilcox was

intense. But if it makes you feel any better, he read all your reports, not just the ones that you wrote involving Junior, but all of them. He said he liked the way you had the evidence server set up," Carlton said.

"Yep, he read all your stuff on the Sheriff's Department evidence server too," Frank said.

"Well, okay then. I guess I do feel better."

"By the way, Gracie, Rich asked if you had time to help with a computer issue?" Frank said.

"Sure! Well, after the bazaar is over. What does he need?"

"Old Treblek had a desktop computer. Detective Percy gave them access to the files. Glenbrook or Samuelson, one of them, has been going through all the stuff, but they haven't found much so far. Rich would like you to take over with the computer search, since we're all short handed. They'll get it to you in the next few days."

"I can do that."

"He'll leave the keys to Teblek's house at the station if you need to go there. I told Rich you like to check out the workspace too. Carlton, you still have someone watching the house, don't you?"

"Yes, around the clock."

"It may be Monday before I can get to the computer. Is that okay with Rich?" I asked.

"It's going to have to be okay," Frank said. "With all the extra folks in town for the Bazaar this weekend, our priorities are crowd control and watching for our drug dealer or dealers."

Frank excused himself to head downtown and Carlton reluctantly exited the Suburban.

"I'd have preferred to sit here another half hour but I'd better get back to the station. Don't want to keep the DEA folks waiting. I'll make sure Rich knows you'll work on the computer Monday," he said. "Back to the grind."

I was reluctant to leave the Suburban myself, but we were approaching dinner time, which meant that we'd have long lines at both booths very soon. I went back to work and worked steadily until things wrapped up for the day. We cleaned up, packed up, and headed first to the Bistro and then home. When we got home, both Max and I collapsed in the family room.

"I think I'm getting too old for this, Max."

"Me too. Maybe next year we'll have Wylie and John lead the Bazaar team. Jacob too. He's ready to do that."

Max got up to get us some iced tea and I checked my phone. I hadn't looked at it since my break before supper. There was a text message from Lieutenant Richardson, "Can Glenbrook deliver Treblek's computer to your house this weekend?"

After rejecting all my initial responses to his question, I compromised and texted, "He can do that, but I won't have time to look at the computer until Monday."

Richardson texted back, "That's okay. We just want it in a secure spot. Carlton may have to pull his deputies off guard duty at the house, so be careful if you go there."

My home office was certainly secure. For one thing the metal access door to the office is in the pantry, a fluke caused when attempting to solve remodeling issues in a quirky old house. However, that solution meant the office door isn't obvious to a casual observer. Max also invested in a metal grill over the window and an industrial grade security system for our house.

The rest of the weekend was a big blur. Max and I worked at the Bazaar from dawn to well after dark. When Glenbrook messaged that he was going to deliver Treblek's computer, I had to call Lucy and ask her to meet him at the house to receive it.

By seven o'clock Sunday evening, we were all ready to wrap things up. Maggie stopped by our booths as we were packing up. She looked frazzled.

"I'm so glad this is over. I don't think I could survive another minute," Maggie said.

"Well, it all turned out great. We had a good crowd. It looks like everyone did a good business. I know we did."

"I was worried we'd have a problem. All the drug stuff happening the past few weeks. I was glad we had so many police officers patrolling the grounds. It made me feel a lot safer."

"It made me feel better too," I said. "I must admit I was a little anxious myself."

"The parking lot has cleared out except for vendor vehicles. The clean up crew is doing their first pass right now. Jeremiah says he's got a crew scheduled for tomorrow morning to do a second sweep of the grounds. It's his church group. I may stop by to help," Maggie said.

"You know Jeremiah will do a good job with clean up. He always has. You don't have to worry. You should stay home and rest tomorrow. You've put in more than your fair share of time."

"I guess you're right. I already canvased the vendors," Maggie said.

"I'll bet they were all happy with their sales."

"They were. I think I'm just getting too old for this. I can't handle the stress anymore."

"With Stan's health problems on top of the bazaar issues, you've had a lot on your plate."

Maggie and I talked a little longer. I think I finally had her convinced to take a day off. I felt like taking a day off myself.

When Max and I got home, all I could think about was crawling in bed. I stuck my head in my home office long enough to verify that Treblek's computer was there and then headed to my bedroom to change into pajamas.

When I pulled out my cell phone to set a wake-up alarm, I noticed there was a missed call. It was from Cory Blackburn. As much as I wanted to talk to Cory, I realized it was way too late to return his call. That would have to wait until morning.

Whether I was overly tired or anxious about what Cory might say, my sleep was restless. Max got up before dawn as usual and I decided to get up too. Max was in a good mood and full of energy as usual. I dragged my body out of bed and stumbled to the kitchen in search of caffeine as usual.

Since it was too early to call Cory, I went to my office and cleared a spot on my work table so I could set up Vance's computer. After that was done, it was still early. I showered and dressed for the day. My plan was to concentrate on the computer all morning and then start on tallying up sales versus costs for our bazaar booths. We never expected to make a huge profit given the price of our two extra large booths, but it all went to a good cause so we were happy if we broke even. Most years we did much better than that.

When nine o'clock rolled around, I decided that was a civilized enough hour to call someone. I dialed Cory Blackburn's number. The phone rang and rang, but he didn't answer. The call went to voice mail, so I left a brief message apologizing for not returning his call sooner and told him to call back when he had a minute. Then I waited.

Several cups of coffee and a couple hours of wading through Vance Treblek's files earned me no useful information on that score. I was debating about calling Cory again when my phone finally rang.

"I'm glad to hear from you. Sorry I didn't get your message in time to call back yesterday."

"That's okay, Mrs. Alderman. I've been in class all morning or I would have called you back right away. Actually, … well... I shouldn't have waited so long to call you to begin with. It's just that I wasn't sure… that is, I was afraid I'd get in trouble again."

"I don't understand Cory. Did you recognize the girl in the photo… Sally?"

"No, that's not it. Well, that girl did look familiar, but I couldn't tell you what her name is. What I wanted to tell you is… well… I'm sorry. This is hard. Do you remember that I told you Candy left some of her stuff at my apartment?"

"Yes, I remember that."

"Well, she never picked her stuff up. I took it to my friend's place along with my things. I got thrown in jail, and my friend put all my things in storage. It just stayed in storage, because my mom and granddad weren't in any shape to retrieve it. Mom had just started dialysis and that was all they could handle at the time. Granddad did pay the storage fees."

"That must have been a rough time for all of you."

"It was, but … well… What I'm trying to say is I forgot all about Candy's stuff. I had too much else to worry about. I hated the fact that I wasn't able to help my mom. I just caused her more heartache when she was sick. I wasn't thinking clearly at all. When I finally got out of jail, I had to get permission to move to Columbia. I got lined up with a parole officer. It wasn't until after all that was taken care of that I was able to get my things out of storage. That's when I discovered that I still had Candy's suitcase and duffle bag. I'd completely blocked it out of my head. I panicked."

"What did you do then?"

"Mrs. Alderman, I was afraid that her things would get me in more trouble. I know I should have said something, but I couldn't stand the idea of going back to jail."

"I understand. What did you do with Candy's bags?"

"I borrowed my uncle's boat and tossed them in the South Edisto River. I'm sorry. Do you think I'll get in more trouble? I sure don't want to go back to jail. I'm real sorry."

"Cory, I don't know if you'll get in

trouble or not. It's good that you're telling me this now. Can you tell me exactly where you tossed the bags?"

"I put the boat in near Edisto Beach Park. Do you know the Live Oak Boat Landing? I couldn't find an isolated spot to dump the stuff there, so I wound up going up the South Edisto River. I forgot how bad the current is during high and low tide. Almost ran out of gas before I got back to the boat landing."

Chapter Eight

After Cory's revelation, I spent several minutes trying to calm him down and then more time trying to pump him for details. What had Candy put in the bags? Where exactly had he dumped them? Cory swore that he hadn't looked inside either bag. He was afraid they contained more drugs and didn't want to know. Maybe he figured he'd have plausible deniability. Cory was able to give me a few landmarks along the river where he'd tossed the bags. For one thing, there was a small island in the middle of the river not too far from the spot. Cory was so worried that he was going to get into more trouble it was all I could do to get him to focus on answering my questions. I kept reassuring him that I'd try to help him out as much as possible.

Once I was convinced that Cory had told me everything and was okay for the most part, I ended the call and dialed Max for some background information and then Detective Andrews. To Carlton, I explained this latest turn of events.

Carlton was silent for a second and then he said, "Seriously?"

"I know. Do you think the bags are still there? He said he weighted them down with bricks."

"They might be there, but who knows what shape they're in," Carlton said. "How many months have they been underwater?"

"Cory put them both in trash bags first. They were fake leather bags, maybe vinyl. That might have helped," I said.

"Just sitting in a storage shed for over a year could have damaged the contents unless that shed was climate controlled. Mold would be a problem for one thing."

"The shed wasn't climate controlled and Cory said he had to throw away some of his things. On the plus side, Max said cocaine doesn't have any nutritional value as far as a medium for growing mold. But it sure doesn't look good for the possibility of finding evidence, does it?"

"It doesn't look promising, but I'd better get on the phone to Rich and Frank. Too bad Junior isn't available right now. We could use his scuba diving skills," Carlton said.

"The bottom may be too muddy to find anything. We've had rain and flooding. But Glenbrook and Samuelson both have diving equipment. I'm sure they'll be delighted to help us."

I was betting they'd complain the whole time.

After I ended my conversation with Carlton, I attempted to concentrate on Treblek's computer. That was no easy task. My mind was all over the place.

At first glance, it appeared that Treblek used his computer strictly for business. His files were mostly spreadsheets, invoices, business letters and an old database. His emails also seemed to be entirely business related. There were a couple of files with pictures, but they all looked to be job site photos. It seemed I might be forced to read his emails one by one and look closely at each of his files. I decided to start with the latest emails and work my way back. I also decided I'd better make a large pot of coffee.

About four o'clock I got a call from my brother-in-law, Frank.

"Rich wants to know if you and your boat are available tomorrow?"

"To go to Live Oak Landing?"

"Yep. Thought you could retrace Cory's route to the place where he dumped the bags. The Department of Natural Resources guys won't be available for a couple days. Rich doesn't want to wait. Carlton says he'll ride with you. The Hardy boys will meet you at the landing, say at eight. They want to dive a couple hours after high tide."

"Okay. Does Carlton want me to pick him up?"

"He'll drive over to your place. Carlton says he'll text you this evening. He's busy trying to get Sunny to go home at the moment. She got wind of the fact that the DEA boys are in town and she's on a rampage. As a matter of fact, I'd better rescue Carlton and Rich. They may both want to leave town after Sunny gets done with them."

Tuesday morning, due to my impending excursion, I got up when Max did. He took pity on me and offered to hook up our extra large bass boat behind the Suburban. He even loaded a cooler with ice, water, and snacks. That was a good thing. I did well to get my shower and get dressed. By the time Carlton arrived, I'd had a chance to drink some coffee so I was at least civil.

"Gracie, I get the idea you aren't a morning person," Carlton said.

"I can be a morning person a couple days a week. However, after being a morning person three days at the bazaar and then again yesterday, I'm all morninged out."

"Do you want me to drive?"

"No, I'm okay. I've got enough coffee in me."

The drive to Edisto Beach State Park and the boat landing wasn't bad at all. Traffic was light. The weather was perfect and daylight revealed beautiful blue skies with just a hint of clouds. We beat Officers Glenbrook and Samuelson to the landing and had the boat in the water by the time they arrived. We had also donned our police vests and loaded our equipment, including a couple of rifles and ammunition. Surprisingly, both Glenbrook and Samuelson seemed to be in a good mood. I had expected them to gripe and complain about getting wet. They, however, didn't complain at all while they loaded their gear in the boat. They seemed to enjoy the gorgeous weather, the boat ride, and were even looking forward to diving in the Edisto river's blackwater.

Carlton had been out in our boat numerous times, fishing with Max and Bud, so he was comfortable with its operation and offered to take the helm. I let him do that so I could concentrate on searching the river bank for Cory's landmarks. After we reached the South Edisto River, we motored upstream. When we rounded a bend, I spotted the island Cory mentioned and then an unusual grouping of fallen trees. I figured that must be the location Cory described and called to Carlton to pull over near the bank. After we dropped anchor, or more like hooked the anchor to a tree root, we surveyed the area. The spot seemed like a good place to dump something without attracting attention. Boat traffic through the week was probably fairly light since it would have been off season.

Glenbrook and Samuelson checked their air tanks and other gear and slipped over the side. They began working the area methodically. While they did that, Carlton and I watched the water and the bank in case we had any nosy alligators in the vicinity. River alligators were supposed to be smaller as a rule, but there are always exceptions. We didn't want the officers to encounter gators of any size.

Time seemed to pass slowly. After what felt like hours, but was in reality less than thirty minutes of dive time, Glenbrook swam over to the boat with something in tow. He threw a trash bag over the side of the boat. Carlton pulled on some gloves and opened the bag up. He shook his head.

"It's just trash. Some boater dumped their trash in the water. Makes me mad. They could have recycled these glass bottles and aluminum cans," Carlton said.

"I know. I wonder how much other trash has been dumped here. It's a shame. This is a great spot. I'm kinda surprised Glenbrook and Samuelson seem to be enjoying themselves. They usually complain when water is involved."

"I don't think they mind being in your boat with scuba gear. It's riding in the Suburban that bothers them. They'd probably be okay if they could wear scuba gear in your Suburban."

I wasn't sure how to take that, so I

refrained from comment.

Carlton continued, "Say why do they call this blackwater? It doesn't have sewage in it."

"I think Edisto is the Indian word for black and it's called blackwater because of the decayed leaves and other organic material in it. Just an FYI, they say alligators like the blackwater of the river."

Another half hour or so of dive time and we hadn't uncovered any evidence, just some shark's teeth. Glenbrook and Samuelson climbed back in the boat.

"It's pretty muddy near the bank. We can't see much of anything there. Have to go by feel. We could have missed the bags by inches and never known it," Samuelson said.

"Could the bags have drifted further down river? We've had a lot of flooding since the kid dumped them," Glenbrook said. "Then again, the tidal current goes both ways."

"You're right. I guess it's a hopeless cause," I said. "I don't know that we'd find anything useful in those bags anyway."

"Wait a minute. Look upstream a little. Do you see those two fallen trees?" Carlton said.

We looked upstream. There were two trees lying side by side with a third leaning at an angle next to them. That arrangement looked similar to the trees where we were moored.

"Do y'all feel like jumping back in the water?" Carlton asked.

"I'm game. We've got two more air tanks. Might as well use them up," Glenbrook said.

We pulled up our anchor and moved upstream. When we dropped anchor in the new spot, we could tell the water was a little deeper.

It was still pretty muddy near the bank. That didn't deter Glenbrook and Samuelson. After a break to drink water and eat snacks, they put on their scuba gear and slipped into the river again.

My cell phone rang. I had to put down my rifle and fumble around to find it. I'd stuck it in a zip lock baggie in my vest. By the time I got hold of it, the call had ended. It was from Max, so I returned his call right away.

"How are things going on the river? Fish anything good out of the water?" Max said.

"Just some shark's teeth and a bag of trash. Why folks can't haul their trash to the boat landing, I'll never know. There's a dumpster beside the parking lot. How are you doing?"

"We're doing great. This nice fall weather has brought the tourists out in droves. But I don't want to keep you from fishing trash out of the water. Bud has a favor to ask you."

"What's that?"

"He says you told him that he should make Ellie's birthday special, since it's her sixtieth."

"What I said was that he shouldn't wait until the last minute to come up with a gift. A little planning ahead would allow him to make it special."

"Well he is planning ahead, sort of. He wants to throw a surprise party and he thought it would really be a surprise if it was at our house. He's going to give her an afternoon spa treatment and then tell her that the four of us are going out to dinner. They'll come over to our house and surprise… everyone will be there for the party. What do you think?"

"I am surprised Bud thought of that," I

said.

"He may have had some help from his girls. Wylie will come over to cook the food. John's going to make the cake, probably at our house, so Ellie won't see it ahead of time."

"I guess we can do that, but I may not have time to get the house in shape. Is he planning the party for this weekend? On her actual birthday?"

"Yep! Tell you what," Max said. "I'll get on the phone to Espy and have her send one of her cleaning crews out Friday. That way everything should be okay for Saturday. We'll have the better part of Saturday to prep for the party. It should work out. By the way, the rest of Ellie's gifts arrived today."

"I'm glad about that. I guess having the party at our house will work. Tell Bud okay. I'd better get off the phone, so I can help Carlton watch for alligators. We've been lucky so far."

While I had my cell phone handy, I took the time to photograph our surroundings and took some shots of Glenbrook and Samuelson when their heads popped up out of the water. I had forgotten my waterproof digital camera in my morning stupor. Normally I keep the camera handy in the Suburban, but I had taken it out to upload the bazaar photos to my computer and it never got put back.

After another half hour or so and another bag of trash, I was getting pretty discouraged about our chances of finding anything useful. Then Samuelson tossed a trash bag over the side that clunked. From the way it sounded, we knew it had something solid inside, like maybe bricks.

Carlton put his gloves back on and

opened the bag up. "Here we go!"

It was a small vinyl duffel bag. Water had leaked inside and it was covered in something slimy, but considering all that, it was in remarkably good shape. The contents were another matter. However, amidst the wet clothes and toiletries, Carlton pulled out something suspicious. It was a gallon-sized ziplock plastic bag with four smaller plastic, brick-shaped packets inside.

Carlton got on the phone to Rich to have a forensic team dispatched. Glenbrook and Samuelson continued their search until all their air was used up.

"If this is cocaine, why would Candy leave it at Cory's house?" I asked. "Why didn't she call him to get it back?"

"Rich found out that much from old reports. He said Candy's car broke down. She called her mother for help and had to have the car towed. The mechanic who worked on it said it was the engine. I guess Candy forgot engines need oil and oil changes. Rich thinks this happened immediately after she went to the bank and stole Cory's money. He also thinks Candy may have been high. Her mother said Candy was acting strangely when she picked her up. Then she got the shakes and vomited. Bea almost took her to the hospital, but Candy begged her not to do that. Candy wound up staying with her mother for few days. By the time Candy recovered enough to think straight, Cory was in jail, arrested for drug possession. Candy may have believed the police confiscated all her drugs."

"Bea never mentioned that to me when I

talked to her. Interesting. If this is cocaine and Cory had more of her cocaine in his possession, that seems like a lot to have. Was Candy a dealer?" I asked.

"Maybe a mule. Makes you wonder. By all reports, she seemed to be short on money."

Glenbrook and Samuelson swam back to the boat and pulled themselves on board.

"Sorry, we need to get our air tanks reloaded. I think we should look around this area some more after low tide. There are a lot of tree roots along the bank and places where a bag could get hung up. It's worth spending more time," Glenbrook said.

"We can get our tanks refilled while you wait for the forensic guys," Samuelson said.

"You might want to get the spare gas tanks filled up too," I said. "That's if you plan to stick around awhile. We've got more than enough to make it back to the landing."

"I wouldn't mind getting some food while we're at it. I'm starved," Samuelson said.

We made it back to the landing without incident, although we had to fight the current part of the way. Glenbrook and Samuelson took off to get some lunch and get their air tanks and my spare gas tanks refilled. Carlton and I waited for the forensic team. Lieutenant Richardson showed up with the team.

After the evidence was turned over to the forensic folks, Rich said, "Those packages you found sure look like cocaine packages we've seen shipped in on boats. They're wrapped securely to keep them dry. Quite a contrast to the other items in the duffel bag."

"If Candy was mixed up with drug

dealers, that could explain why she was having problems and gives us a clue what might have happened to her. They would be very unhappy if she lost a large shipment of drugs. They might even kill her for it," Carlton said.

"She must have realized she was in big trouble," I said. "Why on earth did she leave the drugs at Cory's place to begin with? Was she afraid to drive around Beaufort with them?"

"That might be part of it. I have a theory," Rich said. "From initial interviews with Candy's mother and the tow truck driver, it sounds like Candy was higher than a kite. She might have sampled the drugs, then realized she would be in trouble if she couldn't pay for them. That prompted her to steal Cory's money. We know she took more than a thousand dollars from Cory's account. It was money he'd saved to pay toward his college tuition. A thousand dollars would have been a drop in the bucket compared to the street value of what's in the duffle bag, that's if it's actually cocaine."

"Candy may not have expected Cory to come back to his apartment that soon. He told me he got off work early that day," I said. "Cory's not going to get into trouble about this, is he?"

"We'll see how things develop," Richardson said. "He may be okay."

After Glenbrook and Samuelson returned to the boat landing, it was decided that Carlton and I would go back to Blue River. Rich wanted me to work on Treblek's computer and Carlton was anxious to get back to the police station. I think he was afraid Sunny was there working instead of being home on maternity leave. In any case, we left the bass boat with Richardson and his crew so they could continue their search of the river. Carlton and I headed back to Blue River.

Back in town, we stopped at my house so Carlton could get his car. He headed to the police station. I headed first to the shower and then to my computer room. A nap is what I would have preferred, but I was curious about the files on Treblek's computer. I reread some of the emails and then started looking at his latest spreadsheet.

About six I headed over to the Bistro to meet Max for supper. He was working a split shift, doing the early part of his morning shift and then covering for Rene that evening. When I arrived at the Bistro, I stuck my head in the kitchen to let Max know I was there. I grabbed some tea.

"We've got crawfish etouffee for a special. Interested?" Max said.

"You bet I am. What's the occasion?"

"Ivan and his mom are here for dinner. Ivan's marine buddy is auditioning for a chef's job. We figured if he could pass the etouffee test with Ivan's mom, he would be good to go."

"Etouffee and key lime pie for dessert?"

"Yep, he made four pies this morning," Max said. "I can attest to the fact they're good."

Beside Ivan and his mother, Rosie and Carlton were also at the family table. They were finishing up their etouffee. Ivan's friend seemed to have passed that part of the test too.

"Are you hiring because of the tea shop?" Carlton asked.

"We were talking about hiring another

chef even before the tea shop idea came up," Rosie said. "Jacob Moultry is still taking some college classes, so he can't work full time yet. We do hope to sign him on full time when he's done with school."

"Carlton said you spent the day on the Edisto River. Did you have a good time?" Ivan asked.

"Well, the weather was great and we found some shark's teeth among other things," I said.

Ivan laughed. "I'll bet y'all were there to hunt for shark's teeth."

Brother Bud came out of the kitchen and flopped down in a chair.

"What's the matter Bud? Still upset about wearing a suit?" Ivan asked.

"You're not still complaining about wearing that tuxedo to the banquet are you?" Carlton asked.

"No, he's complaining about having to wear a suit to his wife's birthday party," Rosie said.

"Great! We get to listen to another month of complaints about suits," I said.

"You wouldn't have had to listen to me complain about the tux if you'd gone to that banquet with Max. For goodness sake, you went to Columbia anyway. You could have gone a couple days earlier and attended that banquet. I even offered to do payroll for a whole year. You wouldn't have heard my complaints about the tux and we wouldn't hear you complain about payroll," Bud said.

"Right! We'd get to listen to you complain about payroll … for a whole year," Rosie said.

"Why don't you like wearin' a suit? It's kinda nice dressin' up once in awhile," Ivan said.

"Mom made us dress for church every Sunday. I started wearing a suit and tie when I was three. We also had to dress for birthdays and holidays. I hated it. Gracie had to wear a dress. I doubt she even owns a dress now. What do you say, Sis? How many dresses do you own?"

Everyone at the table turned to look at me. I felt my face turn red.

"I don't own any dresses at the moment. I have an aversion to wearing bows in my hair and hats of any sort, because Mom made me wear either a big bow or a hat to church and on all special occasions."

"See, it's not just me," Bud said.

"You two were spoiled. You spent too much time with your dad, playing around in Gator's distillery or fishing and hunting, instead of doing the cotillion thing," Rosie said.

Bud laughed. "Can you imagine Gracie going to a cotillion?"

"All right, Bud. Enough. If you want to surprise your wife, you need to wear a suit Saturday so she thinks we're actually going to a nice restaurant. And if it will make you happy, I'll buy a dress. We can suffer together."

The other folks at the table seemed to think that was funny. I sure didn't. I hated dress shopping even more than I hated wearing a dress. I was saved from more discussion about apparel when Max brought out my crawfish etouffee and Ivan's friend, Charlie, delivered servings of key lime pie. To my relief the topic of conversation became food and additions to the menu.

After pie and coffee, Ivan left to take his mother home. Bud left to track down one of his daughters and persuade her to wrap the diamond stud earrings he'd bought for Ellie. That left Rosie, Carlton, and me sitting at the family table.

"I think Chef Charlie is a keeper," Rosie said. "We watched him working in the kitchen. He seemed comfortable with the chaos. Ellie said he did well in the bakery. It would be a big help if we had someone who was flexible about where he worked. That's why Jacob has been so good."

"I agree. His etouffee and pie were delicious. We could sign him on a temporary contract right away and do the usual three month trial period," I said.

"Carlton, I'm going to talk to Max about that. I shouldn't be but a minute and then we can head home," Rosie said.

I looked at Carlton. He looked as tired as I felt. "It's been a long day," I said. "Give me a call in the morning. When I was looking at Treblek's files, I found a couple interesting items."

Chapter Nine

Wednesday morning I got a call from the Blue River dispatcher, Melly.

"Hey, Miss Gracie, I didn't wake you, did I?"

"No, I've been up long enough to have a couple cups of coffee. What's going on?"

"Detective Andrews asked me to give you an update. He got called to an accident, so he'll be tied up for a couple hours. There was a fire at Vance Treblek's place early this morning. A neighbor called the fire department. Most of the fire damage was in the area of Treblek's office. Looks like arson. The fire marshal is investigating."

"Thanks for the information, Melly. Has Sunny been into the station today?"

Melly laughed. "No, she's got a doctor's appointment or something this morning, so we likely won't see her 'til later. We've got a pool going. We're bettin' on how many times she comes into the station before her maternity leave is up. Wanna get in on the action?"

"No, but I bet she'll be in every day from now until the end of her leave."

"That's what I'm countin' on. I think I've got a good shot at winnin' the pool."

After I got off the phone with Melly, I took a minute to refresh my coffee. Then I headed to my computer room. Given the latest news, it was fortunate Treblek's computer was moved to my house. I spent another hour or so reading through his files and doing some research. Shortly after nine, I showered, dressed, and headed to town with two items on my agenda, a party dress and Bistro bookkeeping.

Three dress shops and no dress later I dragged myself into the Bistro. I stuck my head in the kitchen long enough to say "hi" to Max and order a bowl of chicken enchilada soup. Then I grabbed some sweet tea, and flopped down at the family table. Maggie Wallace was sitting there chatting with Rosie.

"Hey, Miss Gracie. What's wrong?" Rosie asked.

"I'm regretting my promise to buy a dress. I can't find anything I like. Nothing looks right."

"Why do you need to wear a dress?" Maggie asked. "You have some lovely pant suits."

"I told Bud I'd wear a dress so he would shut up about wearing a suit."

"And we all thank you for that," Rosie said. "Why don't you raid your mother-in-law's closet? Max told me all her clothes are still at the Van Elfin estate. He's trying to decide what to do with them. He figured she must have a hundred dresses, not to mention all the accessories."

"There are a couple things wrong with that idea. First of all, there's a difference in shape. Babs was taller and slender. And second, that's just creepy, wearing a dead person's clothes."

Maggie shook her head vigorously. "No, it's not creepy at all! Vintage clothes are all the rage, especially classic designs like your mother-in-law wore. You don't have a problem furnishing a house with antiques. Why would classic clothes be any different?"

"There's still the problem of size difference."

"I don't know about that," Rosie said. "She just looked a lot taller, because she was so slender. You've lost some weight and I'll bet there's something in Babs' wardrobe that would suit you. Clothes can be altered, you know. Espy's cousin, Alejandra, does that for a living."

"Might as well stop out there and look, I guess. Otherwise I'll need to drive to Beaufort."

"You might need to get one of your dressy pant suits ready too," Maggie said. "This morning Malcom Dewey sent out invitations to a cocktail party. It's scheduled for a week from Saturday. He's inviting board members from the Guild and the Irons' Estate along with some notables from the area."

"Drat!"

Rosie laughed. "Are we going to listen to you complain about parties for a month?"

"At least I won't have to wear a dress to Dewey's party. That would add insult to injury."

"Sorry to give you the bad news. Clinton isn't thrilled either. He and Rene are busy planning their tea shop presentation for the board. Between that and his regular duties at the estate, Clinton's got a full schedule," Maggie said. "His fall sculpture class has started up."

After I finished my lunch, I talked to Max to see what he thought about borrowing some of my mother-in-law's clothes. I was hoping he might object. Unfortunately, he didn't object at all. He even thought it was a great idea. That left me no choice but to drive to the Van Elfin estate.

When I got to the estate's gate, I couldn't remember the security code. While I debated whether to call Max or just count that as an omen and head to Beaufort, the code came to me. Remembering the access code for the house took me another minute or two. In some ways I dreaded the thought of going inside. The stone and log structure had seemed warm and inviting when Babs was alive, but, like the idea of wearing her clothes, I found it a little creepy without anyone else around. Nevertheless, I went inside and made my way upstairs. It was even more intimidating to go into Babs' bedroom, and I really had to force myself to enter her huge walk-in closet.

I wasn't expecting to find a suitable outfit. In all honesty, I just wanted to put off the drive to Beaufort and the hunt through more dress shops. Part of my aversion to shopping was the fact that I didn't want to spend a lot of money on something that would only be worn one time. Trying to psych myself up, I began rummaging through the racks of clothes in the big closet.

Babs' taste in apparel was definitely more stylish than mine and often more flamboyant. One example was a royal blue cocktail dress with a jacket beaded in a peacock tail design. There were numerous other glitzy outfits, so I was surprised to find a simple black A-line cocktail dress with a black velvet jacket in the mix. Except for being a little long, it even fit. So did the royal blue dress. Don't ask me why I tried that one on. In any case, I walked out of the house with not one but two dresses under my arm, along with blue satin pumps and a blue satin clutch bag. What on earth had gotten into me?

Back in my Suburban, I called Espy right

away to get the name and number of her seamstress cousin. My next step was to visit the cousin's shop. Alejandra insisted on doing a complete fitting rather than just hemming the dresses. I've never been very particular with my clothes, but Alejandra pointed out that quality clothes should be treated with respect. I was just glad I had a couple dresses to wear and a promise the black one would be ready by Saturday.

After I finished at Stitch in Time Alterations, I breathed a sigh of relief and drove to the Bistro to tackle bookkeeping. With payroll the next day, plus end-of-the-month and quarterly bookkeeping ahead, everything needed to be kept up. Our accountant would be calling to do an end of month close. With all that, I was also hoping to catch Carlton to discuss the Treblek case.

At the Bistro, I grabbed some tea and went straight to my office to spend quality time with invoices and spreadsheets. When dinner time rolled around, Max stuck his head in the door.

"Frank is sitting at the family table. Want to join him?"

"Sure. I'm ready for a break."

"How about green tomato pie and salad for supper? You could do a taste test on an oyster bake we're trying out if you're game," Max said.

"I'm game, but just small portions. I want to fit into those dresses I found."

Max laughed as he headed for the kitchen. "Can't wait to see you in a dress."

By the time I got there, the family table

was occupied by Sheriff Frank and Rosie.

"Hey, Frank. We hardly get to see you here anymore," I said.

"I know. Jeannie's working nights in emergency the rest of the week, so I thought I'd visit. It's been awhile since I've had one of Ellie's pies."

"Has Jeannie had you on a diet?" Rosie said. "Looks like you've lost weight."

"She's been cooking healthy. Between that and the fact I'm not close to the Bistro and Ellie's pies now, I have lost a little weight," Frank said.

"You and Gracie have lost weight, and I've gained several pounds," Rosie said.

"You don't look any different to me," I said.

Carlton joined us at the table. "What's the special today? I'm starved."

"The specials today are crab cakes with comeback sauce and chicken perlau with pear relish. Max also made some green tomato pies and has an oyster bake for us to sample," Rosie said. "I'll get the drinks and some salads while you decide on your entree."

I got up to help Rosie with the salads and drinks. After we returned to the table, we chatted while we ate our salads and waited for the entrees.

"So any word on the cause of the fire at Treblek's house?" I asked.

"No, Treblek's place sits back off the road. It's a miracle anyone saw it at all," Carlton said.

"Doesn't he have security cameras?" I asked.

"No, there's no security system and no cameras. He doesn't even have working security lights set up around the property," Carlton said.

"That's a surprise. From his emails, it looked like he recently purchased some cameras. Maybe he didn't have time to install them," I said. "I can't remember the date the shipment arrived."

"It's lucky Rich gave you the computer," Frank said. "It might have been destroyed. I don't think Glenbrook had a chance to look through all the files."

"From what Rich said, Glenbrook looked for Treblek's contacts and business associates on his initial search of the files. I think they wanted to get a list of Vance's friends, employees, customers, and other contacts, so they could interview all of them," Carlton said.

"The impression I got from Treblek's ex and from talking to one of his former employees is that he wasn't doing very well business-wise. However, that's not what I found from his spreadsheets. He may have slacked off on taking new jobs in the last six months, but it looked like he was doing okay before that, actually better than okay. He did have quite a lot of money invested in equipment and in the property where he ran his business, but he owned all of that free and clear. It also looks like he sold all the equipment and the property in the last couple months," I said.

"Rich isn't sharing everything with us," Carlton said. "I've known him long enough to know he's holding back. There's something else going on here. For one thing, he didn't jump all over Cory Blackburn for withholding evidence. That's not the normal Lieutenant Richardson I know."

"Or the one I've come to know," I said.

"Let's hope the fire marshal gets done with his investigation tomorrow or the next day. Frank and I are going through the house with him tomorrow," Carlton said. "Want to join us, Gracie?"

"I can't. Tomorrow is payroll day. You might look around the property and see if you can spot any security cameras or maybe a trail cam. I'll check the delivery email again and see if I can figure out exactly what type of cameras he ordered. It looked like he ordered a dozen of them."

"Why on earth would Treblek need a dozen cameras?" Frank said. "I could understand that if he wanted to watch his equipment and his business property. Maybe his worksites. With a dozen he could watch his business assets and his house too."

"But he sold off all his equipment, the building, and grounds that housed his business a couple months before he bought the cameras," I said. "Besides his house, what would he be watching?"

As Max and Rosie placed our meals in front of us, Carlton said, "I think I'll work on Rich some tomorrow. Maybe he already has an idea about what Vance was doing. If not, he's going to want to hear about those cameras. That's for sure."

Between the green tomato pie and Max's oyster bake, I was absolutely stuffed by the time dinner was over. My husband has no concept of small portions. I just hoped that little black dress would still fit by Friday. I should have had Alejandra give me an extra inch, or maybe two, around the middle.

Frank and Carlton ordered pie and coffee for dessert. Rosie and I just got coffee. While the men were eating their pie, Frank got a call from the DEA folks. He left the table and went into the foyer between the bistro and coffee shop so he could hear better.

When Frank returned to the table, Carlton said, "Well?"

"The DEA boys say there's going to be a drug shipment coming late tonight. The drop is supposed to be at Smuggler's Knob. Does that ring a bell with you guys?"

"I've never heard of it," Rosie said. "Is Smuggler's Knob supposed to be around here?"

"Yep, that's what the DEA guy said."

"You've lived here longer than the rest of us, Frank," I said. "If you don't know where it is, who would know? Are they sure it's in the Blue River area?"

"If they know about the shipment, why don't they pick it up before it gets here?" Rosie said.

"They want to find the local dealer," Carlton said. "That's my guess."

"That's it. I'll be calling all hands on deck tonight," Frank said. "I'll see if I can talk to some old timers, maybe Dad. They might have a clue where this Smuggler's Knob is located."

Frank wolfed down the rest of his pie and gulped his coffee. "I'd better get busy. Carlton, I may need some of your guys to help cover the area around town."

With that Frank took off. Rosie looked at Carlton. "Sounds like you'll be working all night," she said. "I guess I'll go home and do some laundry."

"Sorry, we may have to wait until Sunny gets off maternity leave to have a night at the movies."

"I kinda figured that," Rosie said. "With everything that's happened, I didn't really expect to get to the movies tonight. But one can dream!"

I worked on bookkeeping for an hour, then left for home. Since Max was working the late shift at the Bistro, I went to my computer room and looked through more of Treblek's files. About eight thirty, I texted Frank to see if he'd found out where Smuggler's Knob was located. It annoyed me not to know something like that. Frank texted back a "NO!!!"

I wondered if Frank had talked to our old friend, Gator Joe. Of all the old timers in the area, Gator was more apt to know the location of a place called Smuggler's Knob. Before he built his distillery, he was a moonshiner and went around the county trading his 'shine for goods he could sell legitimately. In the case of Rosie's father, Gator traded 'shine for barbecue sandwiches. Gator was getting up in years, so I hoped it wasn't too late to call.

Gator's daughter Imogene answered the phone. After the initial pleasantries, I asked, "I was hoping to talk to your dad if he's still up?"

"Oh, yes. We went to the church chili supper tonight, so he had to sit around and visit with all his old friends. I could hardly pry him away. I'll get him. Just a sec."

After more than a sec, I heard some fumbling and finally, "Hey, Miss Gracie. How you be?"

"Just fine, Gator. Sorry to call you so late. I hope you're doing all right."

"Fair to middlin' most times. Had a good time at the church tonight. Got to visit some old buddies. They're gettin' few and far between, let me tell you."

"Yes, I'm sure that's true. Say, did Sheriff Frank call you today?"

"Naw, can't say that he has," Gator said. "Wait. Maybe that's the missed call on my phone. I've been forgettin' to take that daggone thing with me lately."

"Have you heard of a place called Smuggler's Knob? Frank and I didn't recognize the name."

"You sure it's Smuggler's Knob you want? Not Smuggler's Cove or Smuggler's Club House? There's also a place that used to be near the interstate called Smuggler's Revenge. That was a tavern. Don't think there's anythin' left of it. Buildin' collapsed years ago. I think they finally cleared it out."

"I hadn't heard of those places either, but the location of Smuggler's Knob is what we want."

Gator laughed. "Well, it's a tree, so it's in the woods, if it's still standing. I haven't been through Boardwalk Park in years, so I don't know if it's still there or not."

"You say Smuggler's Knob is a tree?"

"Yep. There used to be a path. It started near the houses at the end of the old boardwalk and cut through the woods to the far end of Baker Street, the very far end. There's that tavern by the cotton warehouse. What's it called? That's where the path comes out."

"You mean The Drunken Rooster?"

"That's the one. That's still open. Old Sam Digby must be a hundred by now."

"I think Sam's grandson runs the tavern now. Old Sam passed away a few years ago. But tell me about that tree. I know where the path is, but how would I recognize that tree? Is it right on the path?"

"Makes me sad to hear that. Old Sam was a great guy. Too many of my friends are passin'."

I gave Gator a second before I asked again. "Does that Smuggler's Knob tree have anything special about it to make it stand out?"

"Well sure! It's about midway along the path. Big ol' Live Oak. One of the biggest on the path. It's got a couple roots stickin' up around it, along with some of those low hanging branches that touch the ground in spots. Ground must have washed away some on the path side over the years. One of them roots is about knee high. That's the knob. There's a hole 'round the backside where some roots and two of the branches kinda meet. That hole used to be big enough to hold a case o' moonshine without it bein' obvious. Say, why are y'all interested in the Knob anyway?"

"I can't say right now. Keep this to yourself. We'll fill you in later."

"Imogene says to tell you that there's a Smuggler's Inn at what they used to call Smuggler's Cove. She sells some of her chocolates in their gift shop. Classy place now she says."

"I'll make a note of that place too, but I need to call Frank right away. Thanks for your help, Gator." I disconnected from Gator and texted Frank with Gator's list of Smuggler places.

Frank called back promptly and started the conversation with a string of expletives. "I tried calling Gator earlier. He never picked up or returned my call."

"He was at a chili supper and forgot his phone. He's old, Frank."

"Right. And I've got my boys every place but Boardwalk Park. Who'd have thought Smuggler's Knob was a tree?"

"I know. Can you call Carlton to cover the park?"

"Yes, but he probably won't know how to find that path. We're already using some of his folks elsewhere. Short-handed as usual."

"I think Carlton knows where the path is. He's had to deal with Elmer Grub a time or two, but I'll make sure and see if I can help out."

"I'll call Rich and see if he and the Hardy boys are able to help," Frank said.

With that Frank disconnected. I called Carlton and we arranged to meet at the station. Then, instead of putting on my pajamas, I dressed in some warm clothes and put on my police vest, badge, and Glock. I grabbed my camera so it would be available too. While doing all this, the thought occurred to me that I was way too old to even consider participating in such a venture. But what was I going to do? Blue River's law enforcement department and the Sheriff's department were short-handed as usual.

When I arrived at the police station, I looked at the crew Carlton had assembled.

Carlton had retired from the Savannah police department so he was no spring chicken. The officers and reserve officers standing in front of me also looked like they were retirement age. I felt right at home.

"Lieutenant Richardson will join us with two of his guys," Carlton said. "We need to watch both ends of the path as well as the drop site. We plan to follow whoever does the pickup. We're hoping they will lead us to their boss. It's unlikely the boss will do the pickup himself. It's too risky. The boss will probably want to check the shipment though."

A couple hours later we were all in position, shivering from the cold and waiting for the drop. Carlton and three of his officers were stationed on the marsh end of the path by the housing development that overlooked the marsh. Officer Glenbrook and the other officers were on the town end of the path by the tavern. They gave me the honor of showing the Lieutenant and Officer Samuelson the drop site. The theory was I knew the path well and could identify the tree. My theory was all trees look alike in the dark; however, by the time we got to the spot we had some moonlight, so the lighting wasn't too bad and I managed to find the big Live Oak. Gator's description was good. The big hole was obvious and, more importantly, still empty. We hid and waited.

Time dragged as we hunkered behind another big tree and watched the drop site. My teeth chattered and I wished I'd bought some long underwear that day instead of getting dresses. And I wished I had them on. After what seemed like more hours, we saw a dark figure coming along the path from the marsh side. I readied my camera, hoping its settings and the moonlight would give me a decent picture.

Whoever he was, he seemed familiar with Smuggler's Knob and he was carrying a backpack. The man stopped beside the tree for a second or two. When he stepped into a patch of moonlight, I took several photos, praying the click of my camera wasn't really as loud as it sounded to me. After another second or two, our suspect stepped off the path and ducked under the low hanging branches of the oak tree, disappearing behind it. He reappeared a minute later without the backpack.

We waited some more. The cold was sinking into my bones. I was beginning to ache. Since I didn't want the light from my watch to give us away, I'd placed it in my pocket so I had no way of knowing what time it was. That was probably a good thing. I might have felt more tired and achy if I'd known just how late it was getting. We couldn't talk either. That would have helped pass the time. We just shivered and waited.

I was beginning to worry that I was going to need to leave to go potty when we spotted another dark figure coming along the path, also from the marsh side of the park. I readied my camera. Our new person also paused by the tree and waited. When he stepped forward, I took more photos. There wasn't as much moonlight, but I still hoped the camera's settings would catch something we could use later.

Our suspect ducked under the oak branches and disappeared behind the tree. Unfortunately, before he reappeared we heard noise, like shouting and cursing. From the town side of the path, we saw a large figure stumbling along. Behind him we heard someone running and shouting. Our suspect heard that too and came out from behind the tree on the run. He had the backpack.

Samuelson bolted from his hiding place and raced after our suspect. Lieutenant Richardson took off right behind him. My knees were not up to bolting anywhere, and sitting in the cold for so long made every joint in my body stiff. I opted to walk down the slope to the path to see what was happening with Elmer Grub and whoever was chasing him. I drew my weapon.

Chapter Ten

Elmer Grub lurched to a stop, obviously startled to see me. He seemed oblivious to the man who was hollering at him from back down the path.

"What the hell! You 'bout gave me a heart attack, Miss Gracie. Wasn't expectin' anyone in these woods this time o' night."

"Don't you hear that man yelling at you?"

The young man in question, Sam Digby's grandson and Drunken Rooster manager, came up behind Elmer huffing, puffing, and shaking his head.

"Elmer, you left your bag with your wallet at the bar. I said I was keepin' your truck keys. I don't want to keep your bag and wallet."

"Dagnabbit! I'm always forgettin' that darn bag. Why my boys thought it'd be better than just carryin' my wallet, I sure don't know."

The young man shoved the darn bag at Elmer. However, by the expression on his face, he must have begun to suspect something unusual was happening. He did a double-take. It must have dawned on him that the person standing in front of him was in the woods at some time past two o'clock in the morning, wearing a police vest, and carrying a Glock.

Even in the moonlight I could see his demeanor change from mild annoyance to outright panic.

"I think maybe I should get back to the bar."

"That's probably a good idea," I said. "I'll just make sure Elmer gets home all right."

Without further comment, the young man spun around and ran back down the path towards town.

"Elmer, how about if I walk the rest of the way with you? You going to your cousin's house?"

"Yep. Wouldn't mind some company. Kinda hard to see in the dark."

I took a minute to turn on my flashlight. Even with that light the trail had lots of shadows. A person had to know the path and be surefooted to navigate it safely. Elmer might have known the path well enough, but he wasn't anything close to being surefooted.

We walked along the trail side by side. In many places tree roots stuck up through the dirt and were hard to see. It was a struggle for Elmer to stay upright. I kept a grip on his arm so he wouldn't fall. He still stumbled occasionally, cursed, then apologized for his language.

By the time we reached his cousin's house, Elmer was so tired he never questioned why I was in the woods at that hour. His cousin, who had apparently been waiting up for him, never questioned why I was delivering Elmer to his door either. I was the only one thinking, "What on earth am I doing out and about at three in the morning?"

After dropping off Elmer, I headed back to where the path came out of the woods, hoping to get some indication where Richardson and Samuelson had gone. I listened intently for sounds that might give me a clue to their location. After a couple minutes I heard faint noises and some talking, not loud enough to understand, but clear enough to know it was a conversation. I headed to the boardwalk.

Carlton, one of his officers, and the two SLED officers were there all right and none to happy. There was no sign of their suspect or anyone else in the vicinity.

"Did he get away?" I asked.

Richardson grumbled. Samuelson shrugged.

"I thought I was right behind him, but he disappeared. By the time I got to the end of the path, there was no sign of him at all," Samuelson said.

"We didn't see him come out of the woods," Carlton said. "Or go in for that matter."

"Maybe he took a side path," I said.

"What side path? We didn't see any side paths," Richardson said.

"They would be hard to see in the dark," I said. "Those paths get overgrown, since they aren't traveled as much. With all the rain we've had recently, they'd get overgrown fast."

"At least Glenbrook and my guys were able to follow the one who dropped off the backpack," Carlton said. "It's not a total loss. Frank's team or the DEA guys will tag them near the interstate."

We backtracked down the main path to the first side path. Carlton and one officer took off down that track. Richardson, Samuelson, and I went to the next side path.

"This track leads to a creek that drains into the marsh. The water is probably high in the creek. If a person had a kayak, they could navigate the creek without any trouble. It feeds into the main channel that runs through the marsh."

It was difficult to follow the path to the spot where it met the creek. Even with Richardson and Samuelson's powerful flashlights illuminating our route, it was impossible to avoid tripping over tree roots and other vegetation. We heard gurgling water long before we arrived at the creek. When we finally reached the stream, our flashlights revealed rushing water. The creek was definitely deep enough for kayaking, but I suspected it would take a strong paddler to navigate upstream against that current.

Samuelson stepped closer to the bank and used his light to inspect the area. "Something was tied up here. Whoever did it just cut the rope rather than untying the knot. There are some deep indentations in the mud like someone stepped here. Take a look."

Richardson moved up beside the other officer. I stayed behind. I was already chilly and I didn't want to risk slipping in the water. The bank was covered with wet vegetation and each step the officers took left deep prints in the muddy ground. To make matters worse it was starting to rain again.

The lieutenant got on the phone to call the sheriff's department asking if they had a boat they could put in the water. Given the hour, the rain, and the meandering path the channel took through the marsh, I had my doubts they would find our man.

"Your suspect could have ditched the kayak at several places along the boardwalk and taken off in a car or truck. For that matter, he could have pulled the kayak out of the water and hauled it off if he had a carrier on his vehicle. Kayaking around the marsh is common. In daylight your suspect wouldn't attract attention at all," I said.

Carlton and the reserve officer joined us. "Nothing on that first path. It dead ends. Did I hear you say the suspect might have used a kayak?"

"That looks like a possibility," Richardson said.

"We can check security cameras along the boardwalk later this morning. I'll see if the boardwalk patrol noticed anything. They patrol during the night, but it's sporadic," Carlton said. "If someone watched for the officers, they could gauge how much time elapsed between patrols. Our officers still pretty much go from one end of the boardwalk to the other, then they circle the park around the gazebo. Once the guys make the circuit around the gazebo, our suspect would be sure to have at least two hours before another patrol, if not more."

"I don't know if it's even worth getting forensics here. I guess we can take the end of the rope, but it looks like a pretty standard nylon cord. Probably too much to hope we could match the cut end with the end still attached to a kayak," Richardson said.

Before we left the park, we explored the other side paths. None of those paths offered any evidence. Richardson did, however, gather some evidence from the second path and photos of deep holes in the mud. When we were done, we dragged ourselves back to the various spots where we had hidden our vehicles. Carlton, being the gentleman that he is, accompanied me to my Suburban.

"Thanks for helping, Gracie. It was above and beyond."

"I'm sorry we didn't catch the guy. I'll see what kind of shots I've got on my camera and get those photos on the evidence server."

"You okay to drive home?" Carlton asked.

"I'm fine. I think I'm getting my second wind."

That might have been a slight exaggeration, but I made it home all right. Having to go to the bathroom kept me awake and alert the whole way. At home, once I took care of my most pressing problem, I made a large latte and plopped myself down in front of my computer to upload the photos I'd taken.

Max stuck his head in the office door about seven o'clock. "So you've been up all night?"

"I'm too wired to sleep. Besides that I've got to do payroll this morning. If I try to sleep now, I'll never get it done."

"Someone else could probably do it in a pinch. I can do it after my meeting," Max said.

"Oh, that's right. You have a meeting with the soccer parents this morning."

"Yes, they want a building with real bathrooms and a kitchen with a refreshment stand. I think they're hoping for some fancy electronics to keep track of games and scoring too. The foundation will likely kick in a chunk of money to help them out. They've worked hard to get the land and get their fields set up."

"I'm all for good bathrooms. I sure don't like porta potties," I said. "I can manage payroll okay, but if you could double-check my work after your meeting, that would help."

Max gave me a kiss. "I'll do that. And I'll drive you to the Bistro this morning and then drive you home after the payroll is transmitted, so you can take a nap. How's that?"

After a shower and change of clothes, I fixed another latte and let Max chauffeur me to the Bistro. That was definitely a good idea. I was okay going in, but after working on payroll for several hours I really began to drag. It was an even better idea to have Max check my work before I transmitted the database material and funds.

As I was clearing the desk off, Frank stuck his head in the office door. "You two leaving?"

"I'm driving Gracie home so she can take a nap. She was up all night running around the woods after drug dealers, if you remember," Max said.

"Not used to those all-nighters anymore, Gracie?"

"No, I'm getting too old for a lot of things. And I'm not afraid to admit it!"

"Well, we appreciate your help. I looked at those photos you put on the evidence server. That guy, the one who got away, looks a little bit like the guy you photographed at the Blue River Tavern. I'm not sure we can use last night's photos with the facial recognition software, but we did get a match for the guy in the tavern photo. He lives in Beaufort. We're going to check him out."

"I didn't think my moonlight photos would work with the facial recognition software. Maybe we can put trail cams around that tree to spot those guys if they try to use that drop site again."

Frank stopped a minute and cocked his head and frowned. After a second he said, "Max, are we still on for a meeting this afternoon, so we can discuss the food truck surveillance equipment?"

"We are. The Bistro can afford the food truck. The foundation will kick in for the electronics."

"Is Bud's cabin cruiser fund being diverted to pay for the food truck? What was it used for last time? An elevator? I'm surprised Bud isn't complaining about it." Frank asked.

Max shook his head. "That's actually what we call 'the rainy day fund,' and the last time we used it was to buy the building next door, so Ellie could have her bakery and coffee shop. Our elevator purchase was years ago. And, for your information, Bud is all for a food truck, so you won't hear any complaints about that."

"No, he's too busy complaining about wearing a suit," I said.

"Does that run in the family, Gracie? I hear you've been complaining about wearing a dress," Frank said.

Max took his brother by the shoulders and turned him toward the office door. "Actually, Frank, Gracie usually complains about you."

Frank paused at the door and looked over his shoulder at me. "By the way, just a reminder, you're signed up for the active shooter drill tomorrow. Be at the staging area at eight."

I just groaned.

Max drove me home, insisted that I eat

some lunch, and then literally tucked me into bed. After a quick kiss on the forehead, he left for another meeting. I rolled over on my left side and didn't remember a thing after that. In college I think that was called a crash and burn.

At supper time son John woke me up. Max already had food on the table, and we enjoyed one of those rare meals where our two youngest children were able to join us. That night I went to bed early because I was still tired.

Even after a good night's sleep, Friday morning didn't go smoothly. I did manage to get up on time, dress in my tactical gear, down some coffee, and head off to the staging area, though.

Once we were all assembled our drill captain explained the scenario. An officer was shot trying to serve a warrant. We had to rescue the officer and get him medical attention as quickly as possible. The leader gave us the go ahead and we took off. I volunteered to drive my Suburban and three deputies rode with me.

The location proved to be an abandoned house sitting on several acres. The ranch-style house, which sat back off the road a couple hundred yards, was surrounded by an expanse of grass. Although there were trees around the perimeter of the property, there was no cover anywhere close to the house, not even a bush or shrub. We could see a sheriff's vehicle in the drive and the body of an officer lying on the ground to the right of the small front porch.

Our leader, a senior deputy, ordered some of his team to go along the outside of the tree line on either side of the property and move toward the back of the house. Then he said, "We need to create a diversion here at the front of the house to distract our shooter, so our guys can get in the back."

I had planned to keep my mouth shut, but it opened on its own. "How about if I drive up to the front door in my Suburban? That will distract the guy and we can pick up the fallen officer."

The deputy scowled at me. "In a real situation, you'd be drawing fire. Your Suburban would only offer you moderate protection."

From the back of the group we heard, "Gracie's Suburban has bullet proof windows and carbon fiber armor. Her gas tank is bullet proof too. I'll ride with her to give cover fire."

I turned around and saw Lucy's boyfriend, Deputy Steven Craig. He smiled and nodded at me.

"I'll ride with Gracie, so we can triage the victim." That comment came from one of the paramedics. I recognized him as one of Max's friends, Tim. A couple more officers volunteered to ride with me. We piled into my Suburban.

Stepping on the gas, I took off, following the blacktop of the driveway and then, when I reached the police car, veering diagonally across the yard toward the front door. Even though I knew it was a fake scenario, my adrenaline was pumping. I had two officers in the second seat and a paramedic and another deputy kneeling in the cargo area by my gun safe.

When we reached the porch, I pulled the Suburban in sideways with the passenger side toward the open front door. We heard gun fire. That was unsettling even though I knew the shooter wasn't using real bullets. Two officers jumped out of the Suburban on the driver's side and ran to either end of the vehicle. When I was in position, I gave cover fire while they made a dash to the porch. The other officer and the paramedic jumped out of the back of the Suburban and ran to the downed officer.

While all of that was going on, two other teams had approached the house from the rear. We heard more gun fire. A third team joined us from the left side of the property. During all that, the paramedic and the officer were able to carry the injured officer to the back of the Suburban. I helped them lift the victim inside. Then we took off back to where the ambulance was parked.

When the training exercise was over, we had to go through a critique. I felt slightly chastised when the drill captain said, "I hope you realize that your strategy wouldn't have worked nearly as well if you didn't have that tricked out Suburban. Some of you could have taken bullets."

"We'll just have to make sure Gracie and her Suburban are with us at active shooter events."

I didn't see who made the comment, but the drill captain was clearly not amused. I kept my big mouth shut. It had already gotten me in enough trouble for one day.

As we were packing up our gear, that same drill captain came over to me. I expected to be chewed out some more.

"How is it that you have bullet proof glass and armor on your Suburban?" he asked.

"My husband is paranoid and has money to spend. He insisted on it after an incident a couple years ago. I had an accident on Twin Bridge Road. The driver of the vehicle that hit me had been shot and the shooter had followed him to the bridge."

"I remember that. A van fell on your truck as you were crossing one of the bridges."

"That's right. My husband said I either had to buy a tricked out Suburban or a tank. Since I didn't think I could parallel park a tank, I picked the Suburban."

The drill captain went off laughing and I climbed in my vehicle to start home. After I dropped off the other deputies at their vehicles, I remembered there was a little black dress waiting for me at Stitch in Time Alterations. I pulled my Suburban out of the parking area, maneuvered it past the police cars on either side of the road, and went to Blue River.

When I arrived at Stitch in Time, it occurred to me that I should have gone home and changed clothes... or at least shoes first. My boots and assault gear raised a few eyebrows when I walked through the shop door. To make matters worse, Alejandra insisted that I try on both dresses to make sure they fit properly. I hated that in the best of situations. It did crazy things to my brain to change from tactical gear and boots to a blue satin dress with matching blue high-heeled pumps. Goodness only knows what the other customers in Alejandra's shop thought.

It seemed like it took forever to try on both dresses and have Alejandra check them. They passed muster so I was allowed to exit the shop, although Alejandra insisted on carrying the dresses out on hangers, covered in plastic bags. I carried the pumps and purse. Alejandra even hung the dresses from a hook in the back of the Suburban for me. I began to think she didn't trust me to take care of the clothes.

After a long and stressful day, it was nice to arrive home to a clean house. Son John was busy decorating Ellie's birthday cake in the kitchen. I ran my cocktail dresses to the bedroom and changed out of my tactical gear, stowing my vest, helmet, and other stuff in the Suburban. The rest of the evening was busy. After dinner I had some paperwork, more like online homework, to do. Max, John, and Lucy got our presents ready and hung some balloons and streamers.

Saturday morning Max and John had to work, so Lucy and I started on the food prep for the party. About noon, Wylie came to begin the serious cooking. He intended to make his mother's birthday meal special and was off to a good start by bringing sausage and shrimp stuffed mushrooms.

We ate lunch on the fly. Lucy and I put out the gifts and finished the decorations. When Max and John got home they set up a portable bar in the family room. John's masterpiece of a birthday cake, with all its icing roses, was placed in the center of the dining room table, flanked by a couple trays of cupcakes. Ellie's presents were stacked on one end of the table.

About an hour before the guests were due to arrive, the kids dashed upstairs to shower and dress. Max and I did the same downstairs. For Max, the process of getting ready took maybe fifteen or twenty minutes total. He came out of the bedroom in one of his good suits and looked great. For me it was an ordeal that seemed to last hours. Because I was wearing that pretty little black dress, makeup was required, something more than my usual eye liner and lipstick. Naturally my hair didn't cooperate, so that meant fighting with my curling iron. After forty-five minutes and numerous expletives, I stood in front of my full length mirror and wondered who that odd looking person was in the mirror. Max came up behind me and gave me a hug and a kiss, so it was worth the effort.

Guests had already started to arrive by the time we got back to the kitchen. Bud and Ellie's two daughters were helping their brother, Wylie, place hors d'oeuvres on the kitchen counter. John was putting together a huge bowl of salad greens and other veggies. Lucy was in the process of setting out dishes, silverware, and napkins. Max jumped into the fray. I stood there at a loss as to what to do. Then the doorbell rang and I knew my job … greeter.

Our house had almost as many guests for Ellie's birthday party as we had for Christmas. When the hour approached for Bud and Ellie to arrive, I wondered why we even tried to hide the guests. There had to be a couple dozen cars parked in our driveway and up and down the road. Still, the guests moved into the kitchen and family room when Wylie shouted that his parents were driving up.

When Bud and Ellie walked into the house, Max joined me at the door. "Come in the kitchen," Max said. "We'll have a celebratory cocktail before we head to the restaurant. We have plenty of time."

Ellie, for her part, acted as if that was perfectly normal. She also acted completely surprised when she walked into a family room full of people. Knowing her husband's past record, Ellie probably never suspected he could actually pull off a surprise birthday party.

The evening was pleasant, except for having to endure all the jokes about me having legs. Frank and his girlfriend, Jeannie, showed up as we were getting ready to sing happy birthday and cut the birthday cake. After we finished singing, I hustled them in the kitchen, so they could get some dinner. While they ate their food and the rest of the guests ate cake, Ellie opened her presents.

I made the rounds with the coffee pot refilling cups. When I got to Frank, he was talking to my brother. "Bud, got to hand it to you. I didn't think you could pull it off."

"Well I did. Two for two. I did the surprise party and I got Sis to wear a dress. You owe me."

"Fair enough," Frank said. He put his coffee cup down, pulled out his wallet, and gave Bud twenty dollars.

"You had a bet on whether I would wear a dress?" I asked.

"Yep! And I won twenty dollars." Bud's big grin changed to a look of concern. "Hey, I had to wear a suit to this thing. Don't begrudge me the twenty bucks."

To say I was annoyed was putting it mildly.

"Don't be hard on your brother. I was the one who suggested the bet," Frank said.

"You both are lucky I'm not a vindictive person," I said.

At that comment, Bud decided he needed to check on his wife. Frank was saved because we were joined by Carlton Andrews.

"So what's the report on the Treblek place," Frank asked.

"We found three trail cams mounted in the trees. One was at the back of the house and there was one on each side. Sunny is going through the footage. I had to let her do something or she would have been tromping all over the Treblek place with us today. I've got to say, those cameras were hard to spot. We really had to hunt for them," Carlton said.

"But you only found three?" I asked.

"Yep, and we really looked hard. I'm pretty sure those were the only ones," Carlton said.

"What did Vance do with the other cameras? I found two invoices for cameras. The earlier invoice was for the purchase of three. The latest one was for a dozen," I said.

"What in the hell would Treblek be doing with all those cameras?" Frank said. "And on another note, the guy you photographed at the Blue River Tavern... we checked his last known address, an apartment near Beaufort. He moved out and didn't leave a forwarding address. We struck out there."

"We're back to square one on the Treblek case unless Sunny finds something," Carlton said. "We did get a break on the drug case. Boardwalk patrol found the kayak with the cut cord. Forensics is going over it right now."

"Let's hope Sunny finds something on Treblek's surveillance videos," Frank said.

Our discussion was interrupted by spouses and other party guests, so we focused on the festivities. However, I had an idea what I needed to do the next few days.

Chapter Eleven

The problem with doing research for our two big cases was other things needed doing first. Sunday, Ellie and I went to church as usual. She was in a particularly good mood after her surprise party, and she and Bud had planned a relaxing afternoon. My afternoon wasn't going to be relaxing. I needed to do bookkeeping at the Bistro and I wanted to check some files on Treblek's computer. I worked all afternoon at the restaurant and then late into night searching through Treblek's files.

Monday morning I got up early and got out of the house before seven, intending to complete my bookkeeping chores early. I expected a visit from our accountant that morning so we could do the end of month close and quarterly reports. I wanted to be caught up with everything.

Laverne Packard Crosby, accountant extraordinaire, showed up in my office promptly at nine, with a blueberry scone and a latte in hand. She smiled and showed off her treats. "I love workin' here. So many perks. And I'll bet y'all are ready to go."

"We are and appreciate the personal service."

Laverne had retired from a big accounting firm when she was fifty and moved to Blue River. She worked out of a home office, and visited her clients' places of business periodically. For instance, when they did end of month close. While our fancy bookkeeping software would have allowed me to do the close and generate our financial reports on my own, we had Laverne come in as quality control. Analysis was her forte and the partners always wanted plenty of that. For example, they always watched the operating budget compared to our actual expenses. With the increased operating costs and the complexity of having more than one location, the Bistro group had been particularly concerned about that for several years. The partners might be a diverse group of individuals, but one thing they all had in common was a conservative streak and frugality. They had the first dollar they earned mounted in a frame by the Baker Street Bistro cash register. Ivan had his first five dollar bill mounted by his register at the Italian Bistro.

After days of filling my brain with talk of journal entries, receivables, reconciliations, amortization and such, I was ready for a break. Wednesday morning I headed upstairs to Max's office with two large lattes and a plan. He had been working on his mother's charitable trust financial reports, so I knew he was ready for a break too.

"Hey, Hon! You look like woman on a mission," Max said.

"I am. You want to take a ride to the country and do a nature walk?" I said.

"Right now? Do you want me to put together a picnic lunch?" Max asked.

"Yes, right now. And a picnic lunch would be great."

While Max fixed that picnic lunch, I cleared off my desk at the Bistro office, grabbed a file folder, and we headed home to change into clothes suitable for hiking. By ten o'clock we were bouncing over ruts on Mill Pond Road, headed to the parking lot by the pond.

After we parked, Max said, "I know there's a method to your madness. What are we doing here besides enjoying the sunshine and fresh air?"

"Vance Treblek bought a dozen trail cams. Carlton hasn't found them anywhere. When I looked through Vance's computer files, I found a couple folders with pictures. At first I thought they were all job site photos, but then I realized something was off. There were a lot of photos of tree lines, woods, and individual trees. What really caught my attention was the location of one of the photos. It was Miller's pond. I wondered if Treblek placed the cameras around the pond. He was here two days prior to the Thursday when he was shot."

I pulled out my file folder with photos. "See these."

Max studied each of the two dozen pictures. "Okay, Hon. So we're looking for trail cams planted in trees around the pond. I guess we're lucky Treblek took photos. He must have taken these wide angle shots to pinpoint a general location, then the close up shot to show the specific tree. Is that what you're thinking? We still may be looking for a needle in a haystack."

"I know. Let's get the binoculars out. Some of the cameras may be planted up high."

"Not too high. I can't see Treblek dragging a ladder around the pond," Max said.

My thought was to go to the site where we found the pile of cigarette butts, but Max spotted another location nearby. It looked like a group of trees where Mill Pond Road branched to skirt the pond. We walked back to that spot and looked for a tree fitting the one in the photo. At first glance all pine trees look alike, at least when you want to find one specific tree. After several minutes inspecting the woods, we began to see the subtle differences in trees, but they weren't easy to spot.

Fortunately I have a patient and methodical husband. Between the two of us we found our first tree. With the help of binoculars, we also found our first trail cam. I got on the phone to Frank so he could send his forensic team out. Max went back to the Suburban to find something to mark the tree. He came back carrying an old t-shirt.

"Did you get hold of Frank?" Max asked.

"Yep. You know your brother is getting to be quite a potty mouth. He seems to be swearing more and more these days. He never used to cuss around me."

"It's the job. Being sheriff is more stressful than being Blue River Police Chief. He always says he needs a Sunny Collins to act as his Number One," Max said.

"Carlton would make a good Number One. Look at how well he and Sunny share the work," I said. "By the way, I called Carlton after I talked to Frank. He was going to call Lieutenant Richardson. They're probably on their way now. Let's mark that tree and head uphill. I'd like to see if there's a camera near where we found the shell casings and cigarette butts."

Max started to tear the old t-shirt but paused to study it, then he asked, "You happen to know why there are three bullet holes in this t-shirt?"

"We used it for target practice when we were shooting with my rifle. Junior and I put the shirt over a bag of cat litter. I duck taped the holes in the litter bag, but I forgot about the holes in the t-shirt."

Max proceeded to rip the t-shirt into strips with the help of his trusty pen knife. I tied a strip around the tree trunk and we headed uphill following the rutted, overgrown road.

At the top of the hill, I had to stop to think where Junior had located the pile of cigarette butts. Max studied the photos. "I think you may be right about this spot," Max said. "That looks like the right group of trees. Now if we can just figure which tree photo to use, we might be able to spot a camera."

"I labeled the photos with numbers according to their photo number on Treblek's computer. They were probably shot in order."

Max studied the numbers on the back of each picture. "I see the pattern. Date and time. Here's the right tree photo, now where's that tree?"

We studied all the trees. "Vance could have picked more distinctive trees," I said. "They all look alike to me."

Max got out his binoculars and scanned one of the trees. I started to do that too, but my phone rang. It was Frank.

"Where the hell are you two?"

"We're at the top of the hill by the spot where we found the cigarette butts and shell casings. We marked the camera tree with a bright yellow t-shirt. It's right there where the road branches," I said.

"I see the damn t-shirt. My guys are getting the camera down now. I'll be up there in a minute."

Frank disconnected.

"You know it's amazing how good the reception is since they replaced the equipment on the cell tower. A month ago we would have had to use police radios to talk."

"I'm sure everyone in the area is happy about that. Say, I think I spotted the camera," Max said.

He pointed to a spot up in the tree. I zeroed onto it with my binoculars. "Yes, it's a camera."

Max went over to the tree and stretched his arm to reach for the camera. It looked like he was short by a foot and a half. "How on earth did Treblek get it up there?" Max said. "I can't reach it."

"You don't think he actually brought a step stool or ladder, do you?" I asked.

"You say he was here a couple days. He might have been able to drive a vehicle around to this tree. If it was a truck, he could have stood on the bed," Max said.

"That would have left ruts in the ground, don't you think? Should I go get the Suburban?" As soon as I said that I realized that wasn't a good idea. "No, we should wait for Frank before we do anything like that. We might compromise some evidence."

A couple hours later we had managed to get three cameras down from their trees, but we were still hunting for the other cameras. I handed out sets of photos to deputies and we searched the tree line around the pond in teams. There were times I considered raiding the picnic basket, but then we'd find another camera and pushed on. By six thirty that evening, we'd managed to find eight cameras and those were on their way to the forensic lab.

"It's getting dark and we never ate our picnic lunch. How about if we head home?" Max said.

"I'm ready to call it quits. Let's see what Frank says."

We walked in the direction of Sheriff Frank. He was conversing with Carlton. Lieutenant Richardson had not shown up, which was curious.

"Hey, Gracie," Carlton said. "We found another camera."

"That's great!" I said. "We're thinking about heading home. It's getting dark."

"Yeah. We're going to shut it down for the night. It's too dark to see well. I'll send the forensic boys out again tomorrow. We'll keep Mill Pond Road blocked off until we find all the cameras," Frank said. "I'm ready for a break myself… and food."

"What ever happened to Richardson? I'm surprised he isn't here," I said.

"Rich answered a call about a body found in an abandoned house. He's checking that out. The deceased matches the general description of Sally Hopper. The body isn't in very good shape, so they'll have to use DNA or dental records to ID the body. That may take time. And cause of death isn't obvious either apparently," Carlton said.

"You say the body was found in an

abandoned house? Where was the house?" I asked.

"It's an old, weathered structure midway between the interstate exit and Carter's Corner Store," Carlton said. "The house has dark brown wood siding. Hasn't had any paint on the wood in years. Some guys from Ed's Salvage and Recycling Company went into the house to pull out the plumbing and copper wires before they demolish the place. The house was condemned as part of the county cleanup initiative. Freaked those guys out when they found the body."

"I'll bet it did," I said. "So no ID on the body?"

"The deputy who answered the call didn't find any, but Rich and the Hardy Boys will do a more thorough search, I'm sure. The photos Deputy Craig sent sure look like it could be the Hopper woman," Frank said. "The corpse has the right hair color and build. Rich says the condition of the body made him think it was fairly recent. He meant weeks as opposed to months or years. The medical examiner was already on the way when I talked to Rich."

"It's been a couple weeks since Sally quit her job at Bitsy's. Actually two and a half weeks. Could she have been there that long? That's if the body is Sally Hopper."

"Whoever it is, the body could have been rotting in that house for years if it weren't for the county cleanup program," Carlton said.

"On a side note, whoever killed Vance Treblek must know that area pretty well, like knowing abandoned houses. Miller's Pond may show up on maps as a body of water, but it's not named. Mill Pond Road still doesn't have a road sign," I said.

"Yeah! Whoever killed Treblek has been around the area for awhile, that's for sure," Frank said.

"Wait a minute!" Carlton said. "Gracie, you shot photos of old man Miller's calendar, the one where he wrote the names of all his hunters. Do you still have those photos on your phone?"

"I do. Give me a minute to find them."

"What was the name of the tavern guy? You know, the photo of the suspicious guy in Blue River Tavern. Frank, you said he'd moved from his place in Beaufort," Carlton said.

"Matthew Grishom," Frank said. "But I'm pretty sure Rich checked the calendar out."

I found the photos and searched through the different calendar shots. "I don't see a Matthew Grishom. The hunting season is just starting so there aren't a lot of entries so far. If Treblek's killer is from around here, he or she could have hunted Miller's property in years past."

"Do you think we might be lucky and find that old man Miller kept his calendars from previous years?" Carlton asked.

"Judging by his office and desk, I'd say you'd have a good chance," I said. "I don't think Miller throws much of anything away."

"Could I just interject something here?" Max said. "It's getting very dark. We could continue this conversation at the Bistro over dinner. Since Gracie and I missed lunch, because we were hunting for cameras, I'd really like to get some dinner... and soon."

"Right! You guys head on out. I'll wrap

things up here and meet you at the Bistro. I wouldn't mind some dinner myself," Frank said.

"Sounds good to me!" Carlton said.

Max didn't wait to be told twice. He grabbed my hand and guided me in the direction of our Suburban. I certainly didn't argue. I was tired and hungry myself. I also felt a little guilty. It was bad enough that I got myself into these situations. Now I was dragging my poor husband into the mess.

When we arrived at the Bistro, we went straight to the kitchen. Rosie was at the drink station.

"Hey, you two!" Rosie said. "I figured you'd be coming. Carlton called to say he'd be on his way as soon as he updates Sunny."

"I wouldn't be surprised if Sunny shows up here," I said.

"No, she had to go over to the high school. They're having a retirement party for Archie Cramer. With all his health problems they weren't able to have one in June. Sunny stopped by this afternoon to pick up some cupcakes for the party. Got to see that baby again. He's a doll," Rosie said.

"While you two visit, I'm going to fix supper for us. What does Carlton want, Rosie?" Max asked. "I was going to fix some tilapia with shrimp sauce for Gracie and me."

"Make that four orders then. I'll get the salads, rolls, and drinks," Rosie said.

"I'll help you, Rosie," I said. "I'm sorry we didn't hear about Archie's party. We'll have to send him a card and a gift card or something. All our kids had him for government class. He's the only person I've ever heard of who could make government class interesting and fun."

"I sent a gift card from us with Sunny. I signed it 'The Bistro partners' and listed all our names," Rosie said. "Just in case he couldn't remember all of us."

"Don't worry about that. The man remembers every student he ever had and their parents too. He's still as sharp as a tack. I just wish my brain functioned that well. I'm so tired I can hardly think straight. And I'm stiff all over."

"You got a little sun today too," Rosie said.

Rosie proceeded to make four salads. I poured four glasses of sweet tea and picked up our silverware. Then I grabbed a large basket of dinner rolls. We set everything on the table and flopped down in the chairs.

"You do look tired," Rosie said. "Not used to all that fresh air and exercise."

"I'm going to have to get to the gym more regularly," I said.

"It's helped me a lot. I love Kevin's self defense class. Lucy is enjoying the class too."

"I regret not signing up for it," I said. "You know, I think my problem is lack of caffeine."

Rosie laughed. "You couldn't get a latte out there at Miller's Pond?"

"No! I can't believe I only had two coffees today. By this time of day, I've usually had four."

Carlton and Frank joined us and Max came out of the kitchen with our food.

"Okay, Frank. What do you want to eat?" Max said.

"That fish looks good. I'll take that," Frank said.

"Here you go. Take mine. I'll make up another plate," Max said.

There wasn't much discussion as we started to eat. Several minutes passed with the only comment being, "Pass the rolls."

"Any updates from Richardson?" I asked.

Frank shook his head. "Not exactly. Deputy Craig went to the coroner's office with Rich. He was one of the first officers on the scene. You know, I think Craig has potential. A few years ago he'd have had a hard time handling a situation like that. Anyway, Craig said the medical examiner thought dental records would be the quickest way to identify the body. The corpse had some extensive dental work done. The body isn't in any shape to get identification from family or friends. We'd have a hard time getting a DNA match for the Hopper woman. She doesn't have family in the area it seems. You did the background search, Gracie. Do you remember any local family?"

"No, she came from out of state about five years ago. She was born in Kansas. Her parents are divorced and still live in Kansas. If she has family in the area, they can't be immediate. Her boyfriend, Roger Stokes, was her emergency contact. I'll look at her records again," I said.

"We're going through the missing persons database to see if there are any other possibles," Frank said. "I sure hope we get something off all those cameras. We just seem to find more trouble. I'm tired of running into roadblocks."

"How about if we talk about something

other than dead bodies!" Rosie said. "We have a nice meal here. I can get some pies for dessert. Let's pick a cheery topic, like 'Sunny's adorable baby boy.'"

"I'm all for that!" I said.

So we changed topics and finished our entrees. When we were done with those, Rosie got up to retrieve desserts for the men. She and I were abstaining. Rosie was trying to lose weight. I still had a fancy blue dress to wear to a cocktail party Saturday. I headed for the coffee pot. As I was loading a tray with cups, cream pitchers, and a carafe of coffee, my phone buzzed. It was Sunny Collins.

"Gracie, Gracie! Do you have that photo of the tavern guy handy?"

"It should be on my phone, but the photo is on the evidence server too."

"I can't really log into the server. I'm at the high school. Actually, I'm in the teacher's lounge rest room trying to breast feed LC."

"LC? Is that short for Lashawn Collins?"

"Actually it's more likely short for Little Coach. If you could send the photo to my phone, that would help. I've only got so many hands. I was thinking that some of these retired teachers might recognize the guy if he was from around here. Coach thought he looked familiar.

"After I saw the photos you took of the guy by the Smuggler's Knob tree, I thought he resembled your tavern guy. He also looks similar to the guy who torched Treblek's house. Didn't Carlton tell you?"

"No, we've been talking about the body in the abandoned house," I said.

"What! There's a body in a house?"

At that point I heard a baby howl.

"Oh, just a minute. I've got to change sides. It's okay, LC. Shhh! There you go. Okay, tell me about this body."

"I'm surprised Carlton didn't tell you about it? A couple guys from Ed's Salvage and Recycling Company found a body in an abandoned house between Carter's Corner Store and the interstate. They were going to salvage the copper wire and pipes from the house before it's demolished. There's no ID on the body, but it looks like it could be Sally Hopper. I guess the body is in bad shape, so they're just guessing right now. They'll have to get dental records or try to track down Sally's family, so they can get DNA. They're also doing a search of the missing persons database."

"I'm going to have to have a talk with Carlton. Well, ... maybe I cut him short when he was giving me an update. I had to get ready to leave for Archie's party. You don't know how hard it is to wrestle two kids around and get ready to go out... Oh, ... I guess you do know what it's like, don't you. Sorry! I'm just frazzled. I'm anxious to get back to work, but I hate to leave the kids. You know what that's like too, don't you!"

"I sure do. Listen, I'll send you the photo, but one of us could come over and talk to those teachers. You should relax and enjoy the party."

Chapter Twelve

There was no convincing Sunny to get help questioning the teachers. She argued that sending police officers to a retirement party would be too disruptive. Sunny assured me she was going to broach the subject of Matthew Grishom tactfully. When the teachers joined her to gush over her darling baby boy, she'd ask a few questions and show them the photo. With tiny LC in her lap, it wouldn't seem out of place at all, especially since they probably all knew what Sunny was like.

When I returned to the family table with the coffee, I updated Frank and Carlton. They both thought Sunny had a great idea and agreed it was best to let Sunny be Sunny. She wouldn't stay out of the investigation, and interviewing retirees at a party was a better activity than some of the other things she'd wanted to do. At least the interviews would keep her occupied for awhile, and she'd have to write up a report after she was done. We use a FD-302 format, so that has to be done just so.

Max and I finally dragged ourselves home about ten o'clock. I made a point to retrieve our picnic basket and cooler from the Suburban and put their contents in the refrigerator. That could be my lunch … or maybe my breakfast the next day.

After spending Wednesday at Miller's Pond, I was really pushed to get work done at the Bistro. As much as I wanted to find out if Sunny learned anything from the high school teachers, Thursday was payroll day, so that was a priority. There were no messages from either Carlton or Frank all morning. I didn't expect to hear anything from Richardson. The temptation was to check the Blue River PD and Sheriff's department evidence servers, but I tried to stay focused on payroll tasks and my bookkeeping chores. I didn't get a chance to check the servers until lunch time.

When I finally did log into the Blue River PD server, I saw a note from Sunny. She had placed three images side-by-side in her report. The image on the left was a photo of the suspect from our midnight stakeout at Boardwalk Park. The image on the right was a photo of the Treblek house arsonist. The middle image was Matthew Grishom. Grishom's face and build matched the park photo figure very closely. As far as the arsonist photo, the image wasn't clear enough to make a definitive ID, but it was close too. Sunny also noted that Archie Cramer, the retired government teacher, remembered Grishom from years past. Grishom and his mother lived with her parents while Matthew was in high school. Archie couldn't remember their address but he remembered the grandparents' names. He also remembered that they lived somewhere in the vicinity of Grub's Greenhouse. This could potentially be a break in the drug case, but did this prove a link between the Treblek shooting and our drug dealer?

While I ate lunch, I received a text message from Frank. The medical examiner officially confirmed that the body found in the abandon house had extensive dental work done, numerous crowns for one thing. He said they were trying to track down Sally Hopper's dentist. Could I see what I could find out?

After a quick double-check of my bookkeeping to make sure everything important was done and done correctly, I started through my background search material and went from there. A couple hours later, and after numerous interruptions, I managed to find a small claims suit for five thousand dollars against the Hopper woman that had been filed in magistrate court by a Beaufort dentist. Sally hadn't paid for her dental work.

I texted that information to both Frank and Carlton, then I texted an update to Sunny. She texted back a thanks and said she was helping search the Miller's Pond trail cam footage. Hopefully that would keep her busy and out of trouble for some time.

After a break to make a latte, I decided to check land records to see if I could find property belonging to Grishom's grandparents. Carlton was searching for that as well and not finding anything. I decided to use some ancestry search techniques to find out where they lived. I could have tracked land sales and tax records, but that seemed like a long and tedious process. Carlton was probably using that tactic anyway. Instead I decided to see whether Grishom's mother remarried. Of course, I had to find her original marriage license first. I figured she might have divorced or had been widowed if she moved back with her parents for awhile.

Somewhere in the midst of my searches, Max brought me dinner and mentioned he was going to help Jacob in the coffee shop until close, asking if that was all right. I was so engrossed in my research that I barely managed to nod okay before returning to my task. I occasionally took bites of my supper as I worked.

The search through divorce records and marriage licenses in several state databases also proved to be tedious, but I finally found the mother's latest marriage license. Grishom's mother had became Mary Cooper Bellingsly. From there I returned to land records. This time I had more luck. She owned about five acres on a back road between the Grub's Greenhouse and Elmer Grub's farm. I was so excited I had to text everyone concerned right away.

Frank texted back. "On it. Thnx."

Carlton texted back. "Great work. I think it's time for you to call it quits for the day!!!"

When I looked at my watch, I had to agree. It was after ten. I saved my data, cleared my desk, and went looking for my husband. He and Jacob were straightening up the bakery kitchen. I helped them finish up and we headed for home and bed.

The next morning I woke up with a start. It was daylight, not just dim dawn-type light, but full blown daylight. I squinted at the alarm clock and realized it was already eight o'clock. My husband was still in bed asleep. That was almost unheard of for him. It took me a minute to remember that he was supposed to sub for Ivan at the Italian Bistro that day. Max had told me something to that effect earlier in the week, so it shouldn't have been a surprise. I still wasn't used to this new flexible schedule. He spent so many years working the morning shift with Octavio through the lunch shift with Bud, that I just couldn't get used to Max rotating jobs as needed. It was an ideal change for him. He enjoyed the variety that it offered and it allowed him to schedule time for his charitable trust projects. My schedule had been flexible for most of my adult life, so I couldn't complain.

I slid out of bed and got ready for my day as quietly as possible. After feeding my cats their canned food and making a pot of coffee, I sat down in front of my computer to decide what my day's agenda should actually be. At that moment I had no clear idea what to do or where to go next. That's the trouble with flexibility.

I started with a search of the evidence servers. Dr. Sykes had posted a report stating that he had retrieved DNA from the scat found at Miller's Pond. It was human feces. We just didn't know which human yet. Sally Hopper's dentist had sent her dental records. The missing persons database had not provided any other likely matches for our remains. Some fingerprints had been retrieved from the kayak found near the boardwalk by the park patrol. They were running a search of finger print records.

The next report that caught my eye was from Frank's office. The Bellingsly house showed signs of being occupied, but no one was home during the night. The house was put under surveillance. No one had returned to the house by the time the report was submitted at eight thirty that morning.

As I was making my second cup of coffee, I got a text from my brother. "A big box just arrived for you. Looks like it might be a 3-D printer. Are we getting one of those to create food?"

I texted back, "Funny. It's for the Art

Guild."

Since I wasn't sure how to help the investigation at that point, I decided hauling the 3-D printer over to the Guild would be a good way to begin my day. I went back to the bedroom to put on some durable shoes. It was raining again. I found Max was dressing for the day.

"Why didn't you wake me up?" he said.

"How often do you get to sleep in? I think you deserve a few extra hours of sleep, especially after I dragged you all over Miller's Pond the other day," I said.

"I enjoyed running around the pond. It was like a scavenger hunt. Where are you off to this morning?"

"Bud says the Art Guild's new 3-D printer finally arrived. I had it shipped to the Bistro, because I could be sure someone would be around to receive it," I said. "The volunteers manning the receptionist desk at the Guild sometimes wander or arrive late. I'm going to do a pick up and deliver. I may stick around awhile to see if Claudia wants my help installing it. She's set up several 3-D printers before, so she may not need any help at all."

"Why don't you join me at the Italian Bistro for lunch? We haven't eaten there in awhile. I don't have to start cooking until two, but I'd like to get there early. Ivan wanted me to test drive his latest recipes. If you bring your camera, we could photograph the finished dishes for the website and menus."

"I'd even be happy to taste test Ivan's recipes after we photograph them," I said.

I headed for the Baker Street Bistro. When

I entered the Bistro's tiny office, I realized I would need some assistance loading and unloading the 3-D printer. I was huge and heavy. I got one of our two-wheel carts and managed to scoot it on the cart. However, I had to have my brother's help lifting it into the Suburban. We also lifted the two-wheel cart in my vehicle, so I'd be sure to have one when I arrived at the Art Guild.

It was a good thing I grabbed the cart. When I arrived at the Guild building, I found a new volunteer acting as receptionist. She panicked when I asked her to call one of the custodial staff to help me unload the printer. It took me a few minutes to reassure her that it was okay to do that and show her how to do it. She still didn't seem convinced this was proper Guild etiquette. Thankfully, Lamar, our senior custodian, was the one who arrived at the entrance foyer with his normal cheery attitude. His demeanor helped everyone's disposition and I got the 3-D printer safely in the Guild building and deposited in Claudia's studio.

I texted Claudia to see what her plans were. She normally scheduled studio time for herself on Fridays. She called me back promptly. "That's great news, Gracie. I've got big plans for that printer."

"Do you want me to start setting it up for you?"

"No, Honey! I've set up similar printers. Right now, I'm not even sure where I want to put it. I was thinking about rearranging my studio. I need to get another table in there."

"Well, if you're sure you don't need my help, I'll head to the Bistro."

"I'll holler if I need help, believe me! I hope to get done at my doctor's appointment and get over to the Guild after lunch. I can't wait to start messing with that printer."

After I rang off, I walked toward the big entrance foyer to retrieve my two-wheel cart. Lamar said he would leave it at the desk for me. The receptionist had disappeared. As I was about to grab my cart, my cell phone vibrated. It was Carlton.

"Hey, Carlton. How are things going?"

"Well, they aren't. No one showed up at the Grishom place, or I should say, the Billingsly place. I hope we didn't scare him away. Frank's running fingerprints and DNA through the databases. We might get lucky with an ID there. Oh, and we have another overdose victim, a fentanyl-in-the-mix case, from somewhere near Beaufort. Her fingernails turned blue. I guess her skin was a little blue too. They said she went stiff as a board. Anyway, she's being airlifted to an intensive care unit in Charleston as we speak."

"That's not good at all. We need to make things happen, don't we? Say, I'm going to the Italian Bistro for lunch. How about if I swing by Carter's store on the way and see if old man Carter has seen this Grishom guy?"

"That sounds like a good plan. How about if I meet you at Carter's?"

"You could join Max and me for lunch at the Italian Bistro afterward."

"That sounds good too. See you at Carter's."

As I disconnected my call, Malcom Dewey came wandering out of the Guild's big gallery. He spotted me at the receptionist desk and walked over. I couldn't get away.

"Mrs. Alderman, are you volunteering as receptionist today?"

"No, just delivering a new 3-D printer for Claudia Ravenou. I'm not sure where the receptionist went. Do you need something?"

"Oh, no. I was looking for Herb... Herb Fitzpatrick. We got separated as we toured the various galleries. I think he may have gone to the restroom."

"I haven't seen him. I'm just about to leave."

Malcom looked past me. "Oh, there you are Herb."

"Just answering nature's call. Are we ready to leave?"

"Yes, if you've seen everything," Malcom said.

"Why, Mrs. Alderman... Gracie, I'm sorry. For a second I thought you were the receptionist. Forgive my rudeness. How are you?"

"I'm fine. Did you enjoy your tour of the Guild?"

"Why yes indeed. I wish I could spend more time, but I have a pressing business engagement this afternoon. I really should be getting on my way. I'm sorry we can't chat longer," Herb said.

"That's quite all right. I need to leave myself," I said.

Malcom looked a little flustered as Herb shepherded him toward the door. The Guild's receptionist returned to the desk, so I followed right behind the two men and hopped in my Suburban, relieved that there was no further interaction with Mr. Dewey.

Carlton beat me to Carter's store. He was filling his cruiser up with gas when I pulled up. I decided to top off my tank as well. Giving old man Carter some business would make him more amenable to answering questions. I also considered buying a candy bar just to seal the deal. All I'd had so far that day was coffee, and I didn't know if I could wait for lunch. A chocolate snack sounded good.

We walked into the store. I let Carlton pay while I picked out my candy bar. I got one with nuts thinking that was more nutritious. After I paid for my gas and candy, I asked Sam Carter if he knew Matthew Grishom. I showed him the photo on my phone.

The old man scratched his head. "That boy comes in here to buy gas now and again. Didn't know his name for sure. For some reason I thought he was a Cooper."

"That's his maternal grandparents' name. I think they must have left their house to Grishom's mother when they passed. She remarried. Her name is Mary Cooper Bellingsly now."

"I remember her. Why, yes, I sure do. She has MS, you know. Sad thing. Beautiful girl. I'm pretty sure she's in a nursing home. Don't know if she still has that property. It was over near Grub's Greenhouse. No, I take that back. It's nearer to Grub's farm. On a dirt road as I recall."

"That's right. Have you seen Matthew lately?"

Before old Sam could reply, Carlton called to me. "Gracie, come on. Frank needs our help."

I stuffed my phone and candy bar in my

purse as I ran out the door behind Carlton. I was fearing the worst. "What's going on?"

"Frank wants us to set up a road block just this side of Grub's Bridge Road," Carlton said, as he jumped into his cruiser. He peeled out.

I jumped into my Suburban and followed Carlton as he sped toward the turnoff to Grub's Bridge Road.

Just before the turnoff, Carlton braked and pulled his car across the opposite lane. I stopped just short of him and maneuvered my Suburban so it blocked the other lane. Carlton and I got out and put on our police vests and body cams. I hung my badge on a lanyard around my neck, holstered my Glock, and retrieved my police radio.

"Does this have to do with Grishom?"

"Yes, Frank says Grishom started to pull up to the house, but backed out and took off flying. Frank's got deputies following him. They've blocked him from turning right at the intersection with Grumpy's Shortcut. Frank's got deputies coming from the opposite end of Grub's Bridge. His plan is to turn Grishom onto Grub's Bridge Road, so he won't endanger as many civilians with a hot pursuit. I think he hopes to stop the kid at the bridge. It should be covered with a fair amount of water after all this rain, right?"

"Definitely! It's probably rushing water after all the rain we've had. But this Grishom guy seems to know the area. I doubt he'd fall for that trap."

"Frank thinks he's blocked all the other routes, so Grishom may not have any choice,"

Carlton said. "Tell me again, why they call that thing Grub's Bridge. At the best of times, it's a slab of concrete under several inches of water."

"The elder Grub got tired of waiting for the state to put in a bridge. People speculate that he wanted a back door, in case he had a shipment of moonshine and needed an exit strategy. He actually bought hydraulic cement to use because he thought that would work better with water. It's supposed to set up faster. He didn't realize that his cement wouldn't bond with concrete well.

"Several of the old timers said he built a nice wooden frame, but his engineering skills left a lot to be desired. He didn't consider a foundation for one thing. I guess the sides of the bridge cracked and fell into the water almost immediately. The concrete slab sank into the creek bed. People think there must be some gravel in the creek bed, because the bridge hasn't sunk any lower over the years. It's usually okay to drive over if it hasn't been raining too much."

Carlton just shook his head.

We heard noise coming from down the road long before we saw anything. That's the way it often is in the country. It was hard to tell just how far away the car might have been, because it sounded so loud. We could hear sirens too. A black SUV came flying down the road. Carlton aimed his weapon. I got mine ready and hoped I wouldn't have to use it.

As fast as the vehicle was going, I knew it wasn't going to get stopped in time. The driver must have turned the wheel as he braked. The SUV swerved and did a slow motion slide, ramming into Carlton's cruiser and knocking it back several feet. The cruiser missed my Suburban by inches.

Somehow the driver managed to pull his car around as Carlton and I fired shots at his tires. He gunned the engine and took off down Grub's Bridge Road. I was surprised the vehicle was still drivable as hard as it hit. Carlton's vehicle wasn't in as good a shape. The front fender was bent into the tire.

Two patrol cars came flying down the road and managed the turn onto Grub's Bridge Road without slamming into us. It was a good thing. I wanted to keep my Suburban in one piece.

Carlton got on his police radio. He must have been giving Frank an update. I walked over so I could hear what was being said.

"Frank says Grishom turned into some driveway this side of the bridge. He's worried that it's the one that leads to some dirt road that comes out on the right-hand branch of Grumpy's Shortcut. Do you know what he's talking about?"

"Yes, I do. One of the Bistro suppliers lives out that way. That's not a great route to take with all the rain we've had. Those patrol cars might have some problems on that road," I said.

"Frank wants us to head to where the road comes out on Grumpy's Shortcut and block it. I told him my car may not be drivable. He says the road is narrow enough your Suburban should do it."

I wasn't thrilled by the prospect of endangering my Suburban again. As it turned out, Carlton was able to pull the fender away from his tire and we took off in our respective vehicles. This time I led the way, because I knew where we were going.

By the time we reached the intersection of the right branch of Grumpy's Shortcut and the dirt road, it had started to rain yet again; not just a drizzle, but a downpour. When I slowed and put on my turn signaled, Carlton radioed that he would take the lead. He pulled ahead just before we turned onto the dirt road, known as Wizard's Way. After a half mile he stopped. I pulled up behind him. He got out and threw on a rain slicker. I scrounged around for my slicker and boots, put them on, and then jumped out into a mud puddle.

As soon as I joined Carlton beside his cruiser, I could see why he stopped. Wizard's Way was now Wizard's Lake. Water stretched across the road and into the fields on either side. The only indication of where the road might be were the two lines of trees on either side.

"I'm going to guess our suspect has already been blocked if he actually took this route," Carlton said. "Could he have found another tract around this mess?"

"Only if he wants to drive through some fields," I said.

Carlton got on the radio to Frank. After reporting on our road conditions, Carlton turned to me. "Guess what?"

"Grishom took to the fields?"

"The deputies chasing behind him ran into the same situation we have here, a lake. They think he broke through a fence and drove across a field. Where could he hope to go?"

Carlton asked.

"Let me call one of my old friends. Ginnie supplies the restaurants with honey and herbal teas, among other things. She lives on the other side of all this water. I'll ask her if she has any ideas about a route out of this mess."

Chapter Thirteen

Ginnie, or as Ellie called her, the Honey Lady, knew exactly where our suspect headed off road. She lived on that side of what had become Wizard's Lake. She couldn't suggest what path Grishom might have taken, but she gave me the name of the owner of the farmland and his phone number.

I called that gentleman, explained who I was, and explained the situation. The farmer swore like a trooper when he heard his fence was knocked down. I let him fuss for a second and then repeated my query about a path out to Grumpy's Shortcut.

Amidst a string of curses, he informed me that if he was home, he would take care of our suspect himself, since the bugger had to pass by his house and get on his driveway in order to reach Shortcut Road. After hearing his diatribe, I suggested he wait at the barber shop until after the suspect was apprehended, thanked him, and told Carlton where we needed to go. Carlton, in turn, told Frank where we were headed so he could send backup in that direction.

We hit a slight snag before we left lakeside. Carlton's cruiser was mired in mud. He gave up trying to back it out almost immediately and jumped in my Suburban. We backtracked to Grumpy's Shortcut and looked for the farmer's driveway.

One of Frank's deputies was there when we arrived and had the end of the driveway blocked. Since there were deep ditches on either side of the drive, Grishom would have a hard time going around his cruiser. However, we didn't see any signs of Grishom's vehicle. Carlton got on the radio to Frank again.

After a couple minutes, he said, "Frank says they're sending up a drone. He couldn't get any helicopters in the air because of the weather. He's hoping the drone will fly okay and they can spot Grishom from the air."

As Carlton was explaining the situation, it started to pour again. I wondered if a drone should be flying in such awful weather. I hoped it was one of the waterproof variety. As if reading my mind, Carlton added, "Frank just said they'll try to send up the drone after it quits pouring. He says it's waterproof, but the visibility is poor at the moment."

That was putting it mildly. While we waited, I got out both binoculars and we used them to scan the area. There was still no sign of Grishom or his vehicle. I began to feel chilled and wished I had worn long underwear or at least had a thermos of hot coffee handy. Then I remembered I was supposed to meet Max for lunch. I checked the time and called him. I was a tad late.

"I'm not going to make it for lunch. We're on Grumpy's Shortcut hunting for a suspect. He seems to have vanished. He went off road about halfway down Wizard's Way and disappeared."

I explained the events in more detail. Max asked, "Are you sure Grishom headed toward Carter's Store Road? He knows you have that road blocked, and it doesn't sound like he's worried about breaking through fences or driving through mud."

We talked another minute or two and I

rang off. Carlton had been on the radio to Frank again. He said, "Frank has deputies blocking both ends of Carter's Store Road and they've begun checking the houses along Grumpy's Shortcut."

"You know, Max got me thinking. Grishom knows we had those roads blocked. Could he have doubled back and gone in the opposite direction? His mother's house is that way. Maybe we should go back and check Wizard's Way for signs of someone crossing the road."

Leaving the deputy to guard the driveway, we hopped into my Suburban and headed back down the road to Wizard's Way. While I drove, Carlton got on the radio yet again.

"Frank says he's going to have his deputies check the other end of Wizard's Way."

By the time we turned off, it had stopped raining. I was a little concerned that I might get bogged down in the mud, but the Suburban plowed on through. We didn't even reach Carlton's cruiser and the edge of the water before we saw a small tree down on the road and sections of fence knocked down on both sides of the road. There were also parallel gouges in the low embankment to our left and smashed vegetation, which looked to be about the width of an SUV.

I sat there trying to remember the roads in the area. Our suspect could have come out on Grumpy's Shortcut and taken another dirt road to our left that leads to Grub's Greenhouse and his mother's place, or he could have gone the other way to Grub's farm and the back end of

Grub's Bridge Road.

We opted to check the route to the greenhouse, calculating that Grishom probably figured there would still be law enforcement on the Grub's Bridge end of the road. Carlton radioed another update to Frank and he made sure there were deputies checking the other route. After Carlton finished his report he said, "Frank is not a happy man!"

As I drove down the road, Carlton said, "You know, we didn't really know for certain if this guy was involved with either the drugs or Treblek's death, but the way he's behaving he sure has to be doing something wrong."

"I know. Talk about acting guilty."

While we were talking, Carlton used his binoculars to scan the fields to our right. I watched the roadside, looking for signs that a vehicle had driven down the low embankment. We went for a couple miles before Carlton hollered to stop. We saw a vehicle in a field to our right. It was near the treeline several hundred yards back from the road.

"Do you want to try to drive there or are you afraid you'll get bogged down?" Carlton asked.

"Well, ... we might get stuck, but the Suburban will give us protection if Grishom is armed. Considering everything, he's probably dangerous."

I found a section along the roadside that was reasonably flat and gave access into the field. I drove close to the tree line in the hopes that the ground there was firmer. Whether or not that was actually true, I don't know.

When we neared the black SUV, we began

to suspect it might be empty. I stopped several yards back from it. We took a minute to survey our surroundings. There was no sign of Grishom. The rain had stopped and some birds flew into the adjacent trees while we waited and watched.

"I think those birds wouldn't be around if our suspect was close," Carlton said.

"I agree. It should be safe to get out."

"Let me go first. You stay back behind your car door," Carlton said.

Carlton opened his door and got out with weapon ready. I opened my door and slid out. After another check of the area to my left, I aimed my weapon at the SUV. Carlton moved toward the vehicle.

It didn't take long to confirm that the Range Rover was empty. It also became obvious why the SUV was sitting there in the field. Both back tires were flat. The front end was battered and the driver's side mirror had broken off. Carlton got on the radio to Frank while I walked around the vehicle.

The vegetation on the ground around the vehicle made it impossible to see footprints and get any indication of which direction Grishom might have taken. Going into the woods would have been my choice, since it offered cover, and would obscure movement. However, all the pine needles on the ground under the trees made it hard to see if there were any footprints there. I watched where I was walking and meticulously searched the wooded area closest to the Range Rover.

Carlton joined me. "Frank's on his way. He's got deputies coming from all directions.

They're bringing the drone."

We separated by several yards and moved slowly through the trees toward the road. The trees were close together and surrounded by a lot of underbrush. There were broken branches and tree limbs all over the ground so it was hard to tell if anyone had gone that way. Tip-toeing and picking our way along, we watched and listened at every step. All we heard was the snap of a twig or the occasional bird call.

As we made our way to the road, we didn't see any definitive signs that Grishom had taken that route. However, when we stopped at the top of the embankment leading down to the road, we could see one long, deep gouge in the muddy slope. Beside it was a half empty bottle of water.

"I'm hoping that's evidence that Grishom has been here," Carlton said.

"You mean fingerprints on the bottle? Do we have Grishom's prints to get a match?"

"We do now. Frank told me Grishom had a prior in North Carolina. He was arrested near Raleigh for possession of a controlled substance and his prints matched the prints on the kayak." Carlton clambered down the embankment.

Once he landed on the road, Carlton was back on the radio to Frank. While he talked, I continued to scan the opposite side of the road for any sign of Grishom or an indication that he had gone up the opposite bank. I didn't think he'd want to stay on the road or anywhere near it with police cars coming after him from every which way.

"I think you're right. I don't think he

would go in the direction of Grub's farm and Grub's Bridge Road. Grishom's smart enough to know there are roadblocks that way," Carlton said. "Heading this way leads us where exactly?"

"It leads to Grub's Greenhouse and the left branch of Grumpy's Shortcut," I said.

"How on earth do you keep all these back roads straight? Most of them are just dirt tracks without any signs," Carlton said.

"I have a husband and brother who are paramedics. They used to drive all over the area, so they would be sure to know where everything was. That was a Sunday afternoon ritual. We'd pile the kids in the car along with a picnic basket, and make a day of it ... or actually a half day of it. Besides taking our Sunday drives, I'm the one who had to pick up Bistro supplies from our local vendors most of the time. It's not quite as bad nowadays. Many of them have started to deliver. However, in the Bistro's early days, I drove all over the area because of our efforts to source locally."

"Rosie and I may have to take some Sunday drives," Carlton said. "Let's head toward Grub's Greenhouse and see if we can find any sign of Grishom."

We made our way back to the Suburban, got back on the road, and drove northwest toward the greenhouse. Carlton watched the right side of the road. I watched the left side.

"I thought I saw some movement in the trees up ahead, just past the bend in the road. The road bends to the right, doesn't it?" Carlton said. "What are the odds it's a deer?"

"Around here, the odds are pretty good."

I sped up and started into the curve only to find a tree lying across my path. I braked.

Carlton radioed our position, then threw open the door and got out with his weapon drawn, stopping to scan the trees for signs of movement. He closed the door quietly. I got out and closed my door quietly as well, then walked around to the passenger side of my vehicle. That's when we heard a gunshot. Carlton pointed to the right side of the road and ran to the embankment. He scrambled up the slope and took off through the trees. I followed him as fast as I could. I had to use a tree branch to pull myself up the muddy incline. My boots kept sliding back down as I clambered up the bank. When I reached the top, I heard a second shot.

Carlton stopped, waiting for me to catch up. He called to me softly, "That could be a deer hunter. I hope he doesn't mistake us for his quarry."

Once we reached reasonably level ground, I found it was still hard to navigate and hard to see what was ahead with so much underbrush. Carlton and I separated by several yards again and crept in the direction of the gun shots, moving cautiously until we came to the edge of the tree line. The road was empty in both directions as far as we could see. There were deep ditches edging both sides. A short way along the ditch closest to us we saw a crumpled body.

Had some poor hunter stumbled in Grishom's path and been shot?

We inched along the tree line, checking all around as we moved. We stopped at a point right above the body.

"Cover me," Carlton said as he climbed and slid down the slope. He grabbed the victim's shoulders and pulled him out of the water, turning him face up.

I continued to scan our surroundings, relieved not to have to look closely at the body. Every rustle of the leaves or creak of a tree branch made me jump.

"No pulse," Carlton said. "He's got a chest wound and a head wound as far a I can tell. He landed face down in the muddy water, but it looks like fresh blood mixed in with the mud. I'd say this just happened, like when we heard the gunshots."

Carlton was on the radio again. I continued to scan the area.

"Yes, Frank, it's Grishom and he's definitely dead," Carlton said. "Yes, that's near the location, but you can't come that way.... No, there's a tree blocking the road. That's where Gracie's Suburban is parked. You'll have to come around from the other direction. Yes, the Grub's Greenhouse side."

From that point it was a waiting game until Frank and the forensic team arrived. We did check for clues as to the assailant, but found none. The road was a rutted, muddy mess. We guessed he or she took off in a vehicle, and maybe had never even got out of it. It was hard to tell exactly where Grishom was standing when he was shot.

After the other officers arrived it became a report game. When a suspect is shot, protocol dictates that the responding officers' weapons must be checked. Body cams must be checked. Interviews must be given and reports must be filed. The worst thing was explaining to Max why I was going to be late for dinner, especially since I missed lunch.

When Frank finally arrived on the scene, he was not a happy camper. "Old man Carter was right. Grishom's mother is in a nursing home. She confirmed that Grishom has been living in her house. We're getting a search warrant for the house and grounds. Hate to have to tell her that her boy is dead. Doesn't sound like she has anyone else to look out for her.

"Oh, and dental records confirmed that the body in the house was Sally Hopper," Frank continued. "All our suspects seem to be coming up dead."

"It sure looks like Grishom was involved with some bad people," I said. "Likely drug dealers. You said he had a prior in North Carolina."

"Yep! Let's hope forensics finds something. We've still got trail cam footage to check," Frank said. "This Grishom guy had better not have been shot by some passing deer hunter."

"I guess we can't rule that out, but surely we'd have seen signs of hunters in the area, wouldn't we?" Carlton said. "Most people should be at work. It's Friday."

"With all the rain we've had today, I would think even the most inveterate hunters would decide to wait for the weekend. The rain's supposed to stop tonight," I said.

It took forever just to be able to return to my Suburban. I was tired, cold, and hungry, but I was too worn out to fish the candy bar and my purse out of the gun safe. On top of everything else, Carlton had to arrange for his cruiser to be towed. He finally joined me in the Suburban.

"Frank says we should head back to the station so we can file our reports. The medical examiner has removed the body," Carlton said. "My cruiser is on the way to the shop for repairs."

"What a day!" I said.

"I know, right! Here we finally catch up with our elusive suspect and he's been shot."

"Where do we even go from here?" I asked.

"We'll have to wait for Sunny to get through the trail cam videos. Forensics might turn up some useful evidence, but that will take time. You okay, Gracie?"

"I've got a headache. I think it's from lack of food and water. Or maybe lack of caffeine. How about if we order some food from the Bistro and have it delivered to the station? We can at least eat while we file our reports."

"Sounds like a plan to me. I need to check in with Rosie, anyway," Carlton said.

We drove back to town mostly in silence. Carlton phoned Rosie to fill her in on what we were doing. He ordered dinner for us. I concentrated on my driving. It was getting dark and there were numerous critters out and about on the country roads. Sometimes I wish I had a police siren. That could help scare the deer away from the road at least.

When we got to the Blue River Police Station, we found Rosie waiting with our food. Carlton took time to talk to her. I gave them some privacy. I thought about calling Max, but I knew he would still be cooking at the Italian

Bistro. He'd probably be there until eleven or so.

I made an effort to wash up a little before I ate supper. Looking back at me in the restroom mirror was a tired, disheveled old woman. Despite wearing boots and a rain slicker, I managed to get mud spattered all over my pant legs. I gave up worrying about my appearance, washed my hands, splashed some water on my face, and headed to the conference room to eat supper and write up my report.

When I finally got home, I fed my cats, threw my clothes in the washer, and took a long, hot shower. Then I put on my pajamas and curled up in a recliner in the family room with my favorite blanket, and a hot cup of tea. My cats joined me.

I was sound asleep when Max got home. He woke me up so I could go to bed.

Chapter Fourteen

Max was up bright and early Saturday morning. I woke up at the same time but laid in bed debating whether to roll over and go back to sleep or to get up and face the day. Going back to sleep almost won, but I started to think about the events of the previous day and my brain wouldn't let me relax and sleep. I got up, and threw on some jeans and an old t-shirt.

When I stumbled into the kitchen, Max handed me a cup of coffee.

"I think I'll make a breakfast casserole, since both kids will be around this morning. There's no telling what time they'll actually get downstairs, but they can reheat the casserole. What are your plans for the day?"

"I'll let you know after I've had a couple cups of coffee," I said.

My brain was addled. After Friday's frustrating events, I didn't have a clue what to do to help the investigation along. I was sure that there was some work to be done at the Bistro. Cleaning house was always an option, although never my first choice. I thought sitting in front of my computer might spawn a constructive idea, so I went to my office while Max proceeded to fix breakfast.

I sipped the hot brew with my eyes closed. That's when we heard rapid-fire gunshots. I groaned, grabbed my Glock and vest, and dashed into the kitchen.

"Seven thirty seems a little early for Dan to do target practice," Max said as he looked out the window above the kitchen sink. "Then again, we do live in the country, and this is South Carolina."

"Yes, but I haven't even finished my first cup of coffee. I can deal with the rapid fire of an assault weapon much better after my second cup of coffee," I said.

Lucy came storming into the kitchen. "What the hell is that about?"

"Dan's son gave him an assault rifle for his birthday. Dan was so excited about getting his new toy that he was out in the backyard at dawn putting up a target so he could shoot," Max said.

"What on earth was Keith thinking, giving his dad an assault rifle! That's crazy," Lucy said. "That sure explains why all the animals are on our back deck. I mean they are all out there: chickens, goats, Jethro, and Moose. They know to stay out of Dan's way."

John came into the kitchen, bleary eyed. "What's going on?"

"Dan's target practicing!" Lucy said.

"He had to pick the only day in a week I could sleep in to practice his shooting?" John said.

Max looked at me and raised his eyebrows. He must have noted that I had on my police vest and had my Glock in hand. "Gracie, I think you can relax."

I went back in the office and stuck my Glock in its holster when I heard more rapid gunfire and glass breaking. This time I slung my holster over my shoulder and dashed into the kitchen. My family had hunkered down behind the kitchen island. Broken glass lay on the counter around the kitchen sink and on the floor.

There was even some on the kitchen island.

"Is everyone all right?"

Both kids groaned but said yes. Max was up and looking out the kitchen window.

"Dan is on the ground," he said.

Max ran for his medic kit.

"Let me go first," I said as I ran through crunching glass toward the back door.

"Don't worry," Max said, as he came up behind me. "If there were any bad guys out there, Dan will have shot them already."

Max beat me to our fallen neighbor. For one thing, he works out at the gym regularly and has good knees. For another, I took time to check our surroundings to make sure no one in the area was shooting at us.

When I got to Max and Dan, I could hear Dan groaning. "It hurts!"

"Yeah, Dan. I think you have some broken bones. What did you do?"

"After I checked my target, I backed up. Must have caught my foot on a tree root. While I was trying to catch my balance, I stepped in that hole and went down."

"You're lucky you didn't shoot yourself on top of everything else," Max said. "I think we need to get you over to the clinic to check out the damage."

"Oh, … are you sure? Debbie's going to kill me."

My thought was that Debbie was going to have to stand in line. My kids and I might just beat her to the punch. After my Friday, I didn't need to start Saturday like this.

"Gracie, how about if you get the Suburban and drive it back here. We'll get Dan's leg and foot immobilized and transport him to the clinic for X-rays."

I ran to the house. Lucy and John were coming down the back steps.

"Does dad need help?" John said.

"Yes, be prepared to open the big gate, so I can bring the Suburban through to Dan. Lucy, check the animals to make sure they're okay," I yelled.

"Should I call Debbie?" Lucy asked. "She's not at work already, is she?"

"No, she's babysitting grandkids, the ones in Conway," I said. "Try her cell phone."

Broken glass all over the kitchen floor slowed me down some, but I grabbed my purse and keys and flew out the front door to my vehicle. By the time I drove the Suburban around, John had the gate open, and I was able to drive straight back to where Dan was lying.

Max hadn't wasted any time. He'd already fixed a splint on our neighbor's bad leg and wrapped his foot for good measure.

John helped us maneuver Dan into the back seat of the vehicle. It took all three of us to get him safely inside. Max positioned Dan so he could rest his injured leg on the seat and then Max and I jumped in the Suburban.

As I started to drive off, I called to John, "Make sure you get the gate closed, so the animals don't get out."

"Oh, you don't have to worry about that, Mom," John said.

That should have been my first clue.

We wound up heading to the hospital in Beaufort. Max decided that the clinic would send Dan there anyway. There was no doubt he broke some bones.

When we pulled up at Beaufort Memorial's emergency entrance, I got a nurse to help us get Dan out of the Suburban and into a wheelchair. Max went in with Dan to help him navigate the triage process. I parked the Suburban and then went inside to look for them.

I should have realized showing up at an emergency department wearing my police vest and my Glock would generate inquiries. The hospital security guard was at the triage desk when I joined Max and Dan. "Mrs. Alderman, do you need any assistance?" he said.

The guard did look familiar, but I didn't think I'd ever spoken to him before. He must have known Max from past trips to the ER. I assured him that everything was fine. It was just an accident. Then followed Dan and Max back to a room.

"Max, while you help Dan get into a gown, I'm going to see if Lucy was able to get in touch with Debbie and make sure the animals are all right. If everything's okay, I may see if I can snag some coffee and a muffin. Do you want something?"

"Coffee for sure. But a muffin does sound good. Tell the kids to turn off the oven, unless they plan to finish cooking the breakfast casserole."

"They may have to check your ingredients for broken glass," I said.

On my way to the hospital cafeteria, I took a minute to call Lucy. John actually answered her phone. "Hey, Mom. Did you get Dan to the hospital okay?"

"Yes, was Lucy able to contact Debbie?"

"She called her. Boy, Dan's going to get a talking to when Debbie gets home! Anyway, Debbie can't leave the grandkids, but she called Keith. He should be on his way to the hospital. By the way, we told Debbie that all the animals are okay. We checked them over carefully. I told Debbie I'd make sure they were fed and put up for the night," John said.

"Thanks! I appreciate that. I was a little worried that one of them might have been hit."

"No, they're all just fine," John said.

"Your dad wanted to make sure you turned off the oven, unless you're going to finish that breakfast casserole."

"I'm working on the casserole right now. Almost ready to put it in the oven," John said.

"Please tell me you checked the ingredients for broken glass? It looked like there was glass everywhere."

"Dad had the food covered, so not to worry on that score. We swept up the glass," John said. "Filled the dustpan several times. Should I call the glass company or do you and Dad want to do that?"

"We'll take care of that. I don't think it's going to rain for awhile. Say, did you use the vacuum after you used the broom? Glass is hard to get up. Small pieces seem to go everywhere," I said.

"Lucy used the vacuum. Don't worry she was thorough. I think the glass is the least of her cleanup problems," John said.

That should have been my second clue. However, I heard beeping that signaled another call, so I disconnected from John. My other call was from my brother-in-law, Frank.

"What's going on? Why are you at the hospital? You two okay?" Frank asked.

"Oh, yes, we're fine. Our neighbor, Dan, fell in a hole in his backyard. It looks like he broke his fibula and maybe a bone or two in his foot. They're going to X-ray his leg and foot shortly. Say, how did you know we were at the hospital?"

"Jeannie's working in the ER today. She saw you wearing your police vest and Glock. She called to ask what was going on. I'm supposed to be taking today off," Frank said. "I think she wanted to make sure I was doing that. So why are you wearing your vest and Glock?"

"Dan was practicing with his new assault rifle when he fell. After yesterday, I just grabbed my gear automatically when I heard shooting," I said.

"Lord help us! Dan has an assault rifle?"

"Yes, he does. It was a gift from his kids," I said.

"The only thing that would be worse is if Elmer Grub's boys bought him an assault rifle!"

"You had to say that. I'm going to have nightmares! Look, I'll go find Jeannie when I get back to the ER and let her know what happened. But, tell me, are you really taking the day off?" I had to ask.

"Maybe, maybe not. I do have some news though," Frank said.

"I hope it's good news," I said.

"Richardson confirmed that Grishom was both a drug dealer and had a connection to Treblek's daughter, Candy," Frank said.

"How did he manage that? I'm surprised he didn't show up yesterday while we were chasing Grishom around the countryside," I said.

"Rich was in Columbia, tracking down a witness. He got that witness to confirm a connection between Candy and Grishom. The witness also confirmed Sally Hopper was both a mule and a dealer. We don't think Sally's boyfriend was involved, except being a user. He's apparently just another victim of a bad mix of fentanyl and cocaine.

"And listen to this, Sunny found Grishom's picture on a couple trail cams and a picture of his Range Rover coming down Mill Pond Road," Frank said. "We found a rifle and a couple empty gas cans at his house. Between those gas cans and the security picture that looks like him, I'm betting he was our arsonist. Forensics is checking the rifle to see if it's the weapon used to shoot Treblek.

"Dr. Sykes is going to check Grishom's DNA to see if we have a match with the scat. You know, the fecal DNA. I've got the guys going over Grishom's house with a fine tooth comb to see if we can find any evidence of drugs. Richardson is at the house now." Frank said.

"I was wondering why Richardson disappeared. I would have expected him to have Glenbrook and Samuelson around even if he was busy," I said.

"They were all busy tracking down this witness and following leads on our drug dealer. We still have the big boss to find… or the bigger boss anyway," Frank said.

After talking to Frank, I felt a little better. Of course we didn't know who shot Grishom, but one problem solved at a time. It looked like we probably had Treblek's killer. Grishom was the most likely cause of Candy's disappearance and Sally's murder. I wondered if we would find any concrete evidence to link them.

By the time I got back to the ER with our coffee and muffins, Dan was in radiology and Jeannie was talking to Max. She turned when I walked into the room.

"Sounds like you have had quite a morning!" Jeannie said.

"Gracie's had an eventful couple days," Max said. "Hopefully Dan's family will show up soon. We could both use some time to relax before the cocktail party tonight."

"Rats! I forgot about that party. I wish we didn't have to go. I sure don't feel like dressing up and making small talk at this point," I said. As tired as I was, I would be hard pressed to be diplomatic with the likes of Malcom Dewey and his pals.

"John said Dan's son, Keith, is on the way. He's the one who gave Dan the assault rifle. It's only fitting that he should take care of his father!" I continued.

Keith and his wife finally showed up around one o'clock, just before they took Dan upstairs. Debbie had already called me twice to get an update on her husband's condition. Once we got everyone up to speed, we excused ourselves and headed back to Blue River.

When we got home, I planned to flop in the recliner in the family room with my favorite blanket until it was time to get ready for Dewey's party. Those plans were foiled. We found Lucy and John scrubbing the family room sofa and love seat. There were feathers and bird droppings on some of the tables and on Max's recliner. There were some suspicious looking brown pellets in the seat of my recliner.

Lucy looked up, chagrined. "Sorry Mom. When I opened the French doors to check the animals, Jethro and Moose pushed their way inside. The rest of the animals came behind them and they wouldn't leave. At least it made it easy to check them for injuries. I didn't have to chase them down."

I just stood there with my mouth open. We apparently had had a donkey, a dog, eight goats, and a dozen chickens in our family room. I was surprised the furniture was in one piece.

"We cleaned the floor first, so we wouldn't track the mess around the house," John said.

"Yeah, don't worry. We've got this. We'll get it all cleaned up," Lucy said.

As much as I would have liked to run into my bedroom and hide for the rest of the day, I dumped my purse, Glock, and vest in the office and grabbed some cleaning supplies to pitch in. I honestly didn't blame the animals for wanting to get away from the assault rifle. They were smart.

After eating a late lunch, we cleaned the family room until we had to get ready for the cocktail party. By that time, it looked pretty good. Max suggested we call Espy to have her send over one of her cleaning teams Monday to make sure we had everything mopped up. That sounded like a fantastic idea to me. It was all I could do to shower, put on my makeup, and dress for the party.

Even the kids complimenting Max and

me on our appearance didn't revive my energy. Max looked great in his suit and I looked pretty good in my peacock blue outfit. I just hoped I could survive the night wearing those blue satin pumps.

When we arrived at Malcom's house, it was ablaze with lights. As we pulled around the circular drive, we saw that Malcom had arranged for valet parking. I, for one, was happy to see that. I certainly didn't want to walk far in my high-heeled shoes. The valet opened the door for me when we pulled up.

As we approached the front door, it opened and we were greeted by a gentleman wearing a white jacket and sporting a black bow tie. I guessed he was the footman. Malcom had gone all out to impress the Art Guild and Irons' Estate board members.

We were informed that our host had to take a phone call but would rejoin the party shortly. We were directed to the bar in the dining room to get refreshments. That involved navigating our way through a fairly large group of people, not all of whom were board members.

The dark oak sliding doors between the drawing room and the dining room were open. A bar had been set up just inside that doorway. The large dining room table was covered with hors d'oeuvres and surrounded by guests helping themselves.

On the way to the bar, I saw Maggie Wallace. She walked over.

"Gracie. Max. I'm glad to see you both. Clinton is running late. I don't know if I can handle Malcom by myself. He's really pushing the idea of getting on both boards. He wants his new friend, Herb Fitzpatrick, to be on the boards too. Do you know anything about this Fitzpatrick?"

"I don't, but I'll check him out and see what I can find," I said.

"I'll get our drinks. Gracie, what do you want?" Max asked. "Maggie, do you want another?"

"Another Kentucky Mule would be great," Maggie said. "That might help me deal with this."

"I don't want anything alcoholic. I'm already tired. A cocktail would put me out," I said.

While Max got our drinks, Maggie and I discussed a strategy to deal with Malcom. We could suggest giving Mr. Fitzpatrick a chance to move to Blue River and get settled before asking him to join the boards. That was an easy solution. How to put Malcom off was another matter.

Malcom entered the drawing room as we were plotting. He seemed rather flustered. He spotted us and came over. "Mrs. Alderman, how are you? I'm glad you could make it. I understand you've been busy helping the police department."

"I've helped them some," I said. "But I wouldn't miss your party. The house looks great. I see you've added some personal touches. Is that one of your paintings over the fireplace?"

"It is. It's one that I did while I was in Europe. You'll forgive me, but I need to make another phone call. I was hoping Herb Fitzpatrick would be here tonight, so I could introduce him to all the board members,"

Malcom said. "I want to check to make sure he's all right."

"Has he moved into the Newburg mansion yet?" Maggie asked.

"No, unfortunately, that isn't going to happen. Apparently Newburg's nephew is going to move to Blue River. I guess Billie Jean was cleared of involvement in her husband's murder, but she plans to relocate. Too many bad memories here, I suppose," Malcom said.

"That's an understatement!" Maggie said.

"Please excuse me. I need to make that call," Malcom said. He almost ran out of the room.

"I hate to say it, but I hope Fitzpatrick doesn't show up. Then we won't have to deal with him tonight. Am I being awful, Gracie?" Maggie said.

"No, you're not. You're being practical. We need to be sure he's going to be a permanent fixture in Blue River before we offer him a spot on the boards. I'm sure Clinton will agree with that."

As I finished speaking, Max arrived with our drinks. He handed Maggie her Kentucky Mule. When he gave me my drink, he said, "Bea Treblek is the bar tender. She made a special drink for you. It's a Mocktail Mule. Non-alcoholic. It's made with lime juice, ginger beer, club soda and simple syrup. Bea says she makes a lavender simple syrup and a mango one. This one has the lavender. If you like it, she'll give you the recipe. She'd like to talk to you anyway."

I took a sip of my Mocktail Mule. "My, that is delicious. Maggie, I think you'd like this

too. I bet it's good with some bourbon in it."
After another couple sips, I said, "Maybe I'd
better get that recipe from Bea and see what she
wants."

I left Max and Maggie to talk and headed
to the bar.

Bea looked up and smiled. "Do you like
your drink?"

"Why yes! It's really good. I would like
the recipe if you don't mind."

"I've got it on a card here. But... there's
something I wanted to tell you," Bea said.

"What's that?" I asked.

"Well, I heard how you helped track
down that Grishom guy. He was bad news. I just
wanted you to know... Well, I don't know if he
killed Vance for sure. I'm guessing he did, 'cause
Vance was trying to stop him from hurting our
girl. You see, ... Well, Candy isn't dead. She's
been in hiding. When Grishom found out that
she lost the drug shipment, he went ballistic. He
tried to kill her. I got her away and hid her out.
The SLED guy, Richardson, figured out she was
alive and in hiding. He said you found out
Vance had sold off everything and set up a trust
fund for her recently."

"Yes, I thought that was a little strange if
she was dead," I said.

"I didn't tell Vance she was alive at first.
He was so upset about her disappearance I
finally told him everything. I was afraid he'd go
and shoot that Grishom guy," Bea said.

"Do you think Vance confronted
Grishom?" I asked.

"I think he was going to do that, but he
got sick. You see, he's had liver problems for a

207

long time. Too much drinking over too many years. I think... Well, I think Vance set up Grishom. Vance knew he was dying and wanted to bait Grishom into shooting him, so the police would arrest Grishom," Bea said.

"That's too bad. Surely there would have been a better way of handling the situation."

"Vance didn't want Candy to have to testify in court. She's not in the best of shape herself. Between her drug usage and what Grishom did to her, she's almost an invalid. She'll probably never be back to normal. Vance was afraid one of Grishom's cronies would go after her. Candy didn't really know anyone else beside Grishom and that girl, Sally.

"I guess Vance mailed a letter to his attorney explaining his plan. Unfortunately his attorney was out of town when Vance was shot. By the time he got back and waded through all his mail, a couple weeks had passed. He notified Richardson then."

Bea and I talked a few more minutes, then she was called to make drinks for other guests. After her revelations, I felt I deserved and needed an alcoholic beverage, but I stuck with my Mocktail Mule and rejoined Max and Maggie.

"You okay, Gracie?" Maggie said.

"Yes, I'm just tired. It's been a hectic couple days."

"Maybe you and Max should take that vacation. Max was telling me that his brother, Andy, invited you to visit him in Japan," Maggie said.

"A vacation does sound good!"

Somehow I made it through the cocktail

party. My brain was only half engaged with what was going on around me. I guess I made adequate small talk with the other guests. My thoughts replayed everything I knew about the Treblek case and Grishom's killer.

Herb Fitzpatrick never showed up at the party much to Maggie's relief. Malcom seemed deflated. I wondered why he was so concerned about the man, but it occurred to me that Malcom never seemed to have any real friends in Blue River. Maybe he hoped Herb would be his pal.

Made in the USA
Middletown, DE
07 November 2023

42070055R00125